# the FREAK Observer

BLYTHE WOOLSTON

the FREAK Observer

Carolrhoda LAB

MINNEAPOLIS

Carolrhoda Lab™ is a trademark of Lerner Publishing Group, Inc.

Carolrhoda Lab™
An imprint of Carolrhoda Books
A division of Lerner Publishing Group, Inc.
241 First Avenue North
Minneapolis, MN 55401 U.S.A.

Website address: www.lernerbooks.com

Cover and interior photographs © iStockphoto.com/Alexander Den (heart); © BBS
United/The Image Bank/Getty Images (brain).

Birdlike creature on cover, detail from left wing of "The Temptation of St. Anthony"
triptych by Hieronymus Bosch (ca. 1450–1516). Located at Museu Nacional de Arte
Antiga, Lisbon, Portugal. Outline by Bill Hauser/Independent Picture Service.


Library of Congress Cataloging-in-Publication Data

Woolston, Blythe.
        The Freak Observer / by Blythe Woolston.
            p.    cm.
            Summary: Suffering from a crippling case of post-traumatic stress disorder,
        sixteen-year-old Loa Lindgren tries to use her problem solving skills, sharpened in
        physics and computer programming, to cure herself.
            ISBN: 978-0-7613-6212-8 (trade hard cover : alk. paper)
            [1. Post-traumatic stress disorder—Fiction. 2. Emotional problems—Fiction.]
        I. Title.
        PZ7.W88713Fr 2010
        [Fic]—dc22                                                    2010000989


Manufactured in the United States of America
1 – BP – 7/15/10

FOR THE
FREAK
OBSERVERS

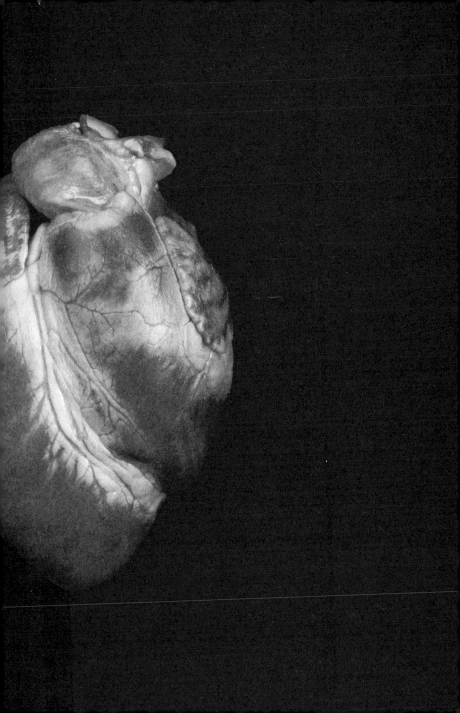

Chapter 1

# Classical Lessons in Pressure and Force

Your beloved physics teacher, Mr. Banacek, likes to sleep on a bed of nails. The effective radius of a nail tip is 1 mm. If there are 4 nails per sq. cm and the physics teacher weighs 100 kg and has 0.64 sq. m of skin touching the nails, what is the average pressure and force for each nail? (Assume that the weight is evenly distributed on all the nails that Mr. Banacek is touching.)

I got up and went to school because nobody said I couldn't. I have a little yellow green blush of bruise under my jaw. It's a nice piece of evidence for the physics of force. Once that energy was distributed along the rubber doohickey on the toilet plunger, the impact pressure was reduced.

I could raise my hand and tell the whole class what I learned about pressure and force when my dad clobbered me. It would reinforce today's concept. I have been observing physics in action, just as instructed. I don't raise my hand. I don't say a word.

. . .

I'm in school, and I'm trying to figure out why my physics teacher wants to sleep on a bed of nails in the first place— and that's distracting me from the math, which is honest and elegant and doesn't require any human motivation. I'm in school, but I don't even make it through my first class before I receive a little note informing me to visit Mrs. Bishop in the counseling office. So I'm sitting outside her door watching first period tick away. I'm pretty sure I'm missing class so she can tell me that I shouldn't miss class. That's the way things work.

. . .

"Loa, come on in," says Mrs. Bishop. "I understand you were friends with Esther." She has to get right to the point. There is only one of her, and there are a lot of students.

What do I say to that? We rode the same bus. We went to grade school together for nine years. I know Esther liked pink meringue cookies.

I have a picture of us from first grade. We are standing on the steps of the school for picture day, Esther, Reba, and I. Esther is wearing a long dress that makes her look like she belongs on a wagon train. Reba has on her favorite Mulan T-shirt and a pink, ruffled skirt. I have a cocoa stain down my front, and I'm trying to look really fierce, so I have my hands curled up in little fists and I'm scowling. I wasn't angry. I just thought it would be cool.

My mother didn't think it was cool. She had forgotten that it was picture day. She would have made sure I wore a better shirt. The cocoa stain was bad, but I made it even worse by frowning.

I remember the first time I saw Esther. It was before we even went to school.

My dad decided I needed a puppy. Esther's family had some, so we drove up to their place. They had pole corrals right in their yard. Their house was even older than our house, but it was a lot bigger too. It had to be big. It seemed to me like there were a lot of people in that family. Some of Esther's aunts and uncles and cousins might have been there. Or maybe my measuring stick for "a lot of people" was my own family, so more than three was a lot.

My dad told me to stay in the car while he got out. He went in the house to talk to Esther's dad. In a little while, the kids had all come out to stare at me in the car. I was staring back. Then one of the big girls went into the house and came out with a can of creamed corn. She poured it on the dirt. A whole bunch of puppies came tumbling out from under the porch and started licking up the yellow mess. Then a big pig came around the corner and headed for the corn. Before he could get there, a little tiny girl picked up a stick of firewood and whacked that pig as hard as she could right in the head. The other kids started laughing, but that little girl just stood her ground. She wouldn't let that pig get close to that creamed corn. That little tiny girl was Esther.

Then my dad came out of the house. Esther's dad pointed at a couple of the puppies. My dad reached down and scooped one up.

Next thing I knew, I was the happiest kid in the world and that puppy was giving me a tongue bath like crazy. He smelled a little bit like creamed corn.

Esther is dead now. She was a defender of puppies and a whacker of pigs, and now she is dead.

"Yes," I say, "I knew her."

"Well," says Mrs. Bishop, "How are you handling that?"

"I'm OK," I lie. "It's sad, but I'm doing OK."

The truth is just way too complicated, and it doesn't belong in this conversation: My dad lost his shit and clobbered me with a toilet plunger, and then I totally lost *my* shit and started hallucinating again. You know how it is. . . . Same-ol', same-ol'.

"I need to tell you that I sent a letter to your parents."

Well, I'd better keep a close eye on the mail, because that is a little gathering shit storm on the horizon. Does

Mrs. Bishop really think my parents are going to read a letter on official school stationery and then sit me down at the kitchen table and say, "Honey, school's important"? Does she imagine there will be hugs and a brand-new graphing calculator, just to show they care?

My family is more about yelling than hugging.

There will be yelling if that letter is read. Some of that yelling will be directed at Mrs. Bishop—"and-who-does-she-think-she-is-the-bitch?"—and some will be at me—"damn-it-to-hell-look-where-your-cattin'-around-got-you"—and some might be at Little Harold if he has the TV on too loud or if he left the bread unwrapped so it will dry out. Oh, yeah, it would be a very special after-school special. I can hardly wait.

"We understand how upsetting this sort of thing can be, especially when you are still working through . . . " she trails off—then gets back on track, "But you have to come to school. We have to keep you headed toward graduation. We like you, but we don't want you to spend an extra year with us."

It's a dumb joke, but she might be telling me the truth. I think she really does like me. I think she really does want me to graduate. I also think she gives that speech to a lot of kids, and most of them end up with a GED or in the alternative program or working some crap job.

"Not that I think that is going to happen. But this is the year, Loa, this is the year that grades matter. The universities will be most interested in what you do this year. Scholarships are harder and harder to find—grants seem like they get smaller every year. So I just wanted to let your parents know the situation. We all need to work together. We need to make sure your grades prove you can make it." She shifts gears a little, rummages around in one of the piles on her desk.

"I also wanted to give you this. Another student was considering this school. It seems like a good fit for you. And this one too." She is collecting some bright and shiny booklets and pamphlets in her hand. "You need to start thinking about applying to schools. There is a meeting about the financial aid process during your lunch period next week. You need to go. Listen for the announcement. And you should probably get back on track with speech and debate. Activities like that make a difference when they look at your application."

"I lost my debate partner," I say.

"Ah, yes, you were on a team with Corey." She pauses a little. Her face is resting in just a little bit of a smile. The worry lines fade out of her forehead. "What a great opportunity for him."

"A great opportunity," I agree. Repetition always sounds like agreement unless you make it sound like a question.

"You could try an individual event like Lincoln-Douglas or Impromptu. Corey used to do Impromptu before the two of you teamed up for debate."

There are at least seven good reasons why I would suck at Impromptu, but I have the answer that trumps all answers.

"I have to work. I work after school and on the weekends now, so practice and traveling to meets is out."

"Oh. I'd forgotten."

Did she know? I never told her. Is she supposed to know everything about every student?

"Well, that's good too."

She is unstoppable.

"Working to save money for college shows real responsibility."

I think we spent my last check on toilet paper, wool socks, and gas. A college fund is a little low on the list of priorities right now—below laundry detergent, actually, and way below the power bill. This is a situation where the best answer is a nod.

Things are wrapping up. She scribbles out a hall pass and late excuse for me. "Take care, Loa."

Now I get to take my note and slither into French.

. . .

*"Lulu! Voozetahnretahr."*

*"Maywe, juhzsweearetard."* I should get points for honesty too.

. . .

I missed school. I'm entitled to make up the work, because death is a good excuse.

In French I get a ziplock bag full of mini-tapes and a crappy little tape player. *Voila, c'est facile*—or, as I like to say, *Wallasayfasill.*

In math all I need to do is adjust the dates on the syllabus. Each missed assignment is now due one week later.

There are no daily assignments in computing. I either turn my programs and web page in by the last week of term or I fail. I could probably do everything in one sleepless code-monkey marathon if I had access to a computer for more than forty-five minutes a school day. Anyway, not to worry. I have that covered.

In English, Miss (Heartless) Hart says there is no way to make up for the missed discussions in class. Have I kept up with the reading schedule? I would like to point out that I could keep up with her reading schedule even if I had to reinvent the alphabet on a daily basis before I got started. I don't point that out. I just bask in her glare.

During lunch I revisit Mr. Banacek in physics.

"You can just pull something out of the extra-credit jar," he says. So I reach in and fish out a scrap of paper. It says:

### Freak Observer (Boltzmann Brain)

"Write me something, and get it to me by the end of the quarter. OK, Loa?" He looks like he knows he should say something kind.

"I have to hurry. I'll miss my class," I say, to make it easier for both of us.

· · ·

It is hard riding the bus home. I take a seat behind J.B. the driver and plug the taped French lessons into my head. It's my only defense against the inevitable. And it won't work, because the inevitable is inevitable.

The bus goes right by the place where Esther died.

It was bad in the morning when I was going to school, but it is worse now in the afternoon, because I know it is going to happen. Shutting my eyes and pretending French is a language isn't going to help. Nothing is going to help.

# Chapter 2

## Conservation of Energy

After an accident on a straight, level stretch of blacktop road, a trooper measures the skid marks and finds they are 100 feet long. The vehicle involved weighs 2,050 pounds. If the speed limit is 60 mph, does the trooper have enough information to cite the driver for speeding? Why or why not?

This is how it happened.

The trooper was nice. He let me ride in the front seat. He pulled out a box of some industrial-grade tissues when he saw me wiping my snot on my sleeve.

Then he said, "I'm sorry. I have to take you home. It's the law."

When he said it, I believed him. And I felt a little sorry for him, because troopers have to do a lot of things that are terrible, like being where death happens. It's just part of their job. They arrive and they decide who is alive and who is dead and who is responsible. They talk on their radios, and they talk to the ones left living, and sometimes they take people home—even and especially if they don't want to go home.

The troopers weren't the first ones at the scene. The truck driver was there. I and Abel were both there. And Esther's body was there. I don't know who called the troopers, but I remember the sirens seemed to start almost as soon as I could figure out what had happened.

I hadn't even been looking at Esther. I was watching the river current and thinking about how the water looked almost predictable when it broke around the rocks into rapids. I know about chaos physics. I know the breaking point of a riffle around a rock is no more predictable than the way wind sculpts a cloud. I know that, but it didn't stop me from trying to see the pattern. So I was neglecting Esther. If she had invited me to come along so she would have had someone to talk to, I was a bad choice. I was all burrowed into my brain.

The last I saw her, she was standing at the top of the cutbank. What she was thinking then or what she was thinking when she ran down the bank, I do not know. I told them that.

I heard tires squeal.

I heard a crash that went on and on.

By the time I ran partway down the bank toward the highway, the logging truck was jackknifed at the bottom of the hill. His load had broken loose, and some of the logs were still shifting, still moving to the place gravity wanted them to be. One of them had shot way down the road and shattered on impact. Velocity. Acceleration. Linear momentum.

It amazed me. Like WOW! Look at that tree exploded to splinters—an origami shooting star.

The trucker had his door open and was kneeling on the pavement. He was pretty lucky to have got out of that mess still walking. One of his logs could have moved right through him on its trajectory. I could hear him yelling, but I couldn't figure out what he was saying. It was kind of broken up and hard to understand because he was puking. He was still trying to say something, but the words were lost in gagging and spitting.

I was so distracted by that guy that I didn't see the rest of the picture right away.

Then I saw Esther.

My first thought was

*Her heart has fallen out of her body.*

I didn't know that could happen. I didn't know what to do. So I just froze there on the cutbank.

*I don't know how to put a heart back into a body.*

It was the only thought I had, and it wasn't very useful.

It seemed like a long time, but it wasn't really, because Abel was right behind me, and he pushed me out of the way. I slid down the bank in the loose dirt and rocks. Then I just sat there where I fell. I watched Abel while he grabbed his sister and tried to make her be alive.

I could see that her heart hadn't fallen out. The muscle on her arm had been torn away from the bone. It was just a lump of muscle. Her heart was safe inside her, but she was still dead.

I didn't go to her. I was afraid to go down the bank and onto the highway. I was afraid to look and I was afraid to see.

I wasn't a very good friend.

I guess I could have touched her hand or said her name. I didn't. Maybe that's the sort of thing I will regret for the rest of my life. I don't know. So far the rest of my life hasn't been very long.

. . .

The troopers came with their sirens and flashing lights. They put flares in the road so the accident wouldn't get worse. Pretty soon it was dark, and the paramedics came and gathered Esther up and took her away. Abel went too. They didn't use the siren when they drove away. It was that silent ambulance that got me. I might have been OK if it hadn't been for that quiet ambulance.

A trooper came and led me to his car. I answered all his questions, but I don't think my answers were much use: It was just the three of us so far; the others weren't there yet; we hadn't been drinking because there wasn't anything to drink; we were waiting. Abel was sitting in the cab smoking—just Marlboros. I was sitting on the tailgate, staring at the river. I don't know what was going on with Esther.

"There are two kinds of people," said the trooper, "The ones who run toward the accident and the ones who run away." I think he was trying to console me or help me not feel guilty.

Then he said it was time to get me home. The clock on the dashboard of the cruiser said it was 10:37.

The headlights of the trooper's car carved little cones of visibility in the night. It was a very dark world. The river beside the road was blacker than the riverbanks. The trees were darker than the sky. The stars were little and far away. I watched them, and I watched the reflectors on the mile markers. The stars and the reflectors seemed pretty pathetic in the middle of all that night.

We were going to be at my turnoff soon. I didn't say anything. If I stayed quiet, the trooper might just keep driving on and on, up the valley, past the subdivisions and the old ranches.

It was a silly idea. Troopers know where the roads are. I had told him my name and address during the questioning. He knew where to turn away from the blacktop and which dirt road led to my house. I wish we lived deeper up the canyon, but we're not that far from the main road. It is just too little time to get my shit together. The road curves around the old pasture fence. There is our barn where nothing lives anymore. The house huddles in the dark, smaller than the barn and almost as empty.

Thin grey light escapes the windows of the kitchen and bathroom. I know the trooper is going to that door, the back door, in the middle of the scabbed-on addition to the main house. The real front door faces the creek because the house turns its back on the road. Nothing good ever comes from that direction. That's what the house seems to believe.

The trooper left the engine running while he went to the door. I don't know if they aren't allowed to turn off the engine or if he just wanted me to feel warm and safe. Or maybe he did it so I couldn't hear what he and my dad were saying on the back porch.

I couldn't pay attention anyway. It took everything just to keep my eyes open. I didn't want them shut. My imagination kicks in when I close my eyes.

Next thing I knew, the trooper was opening the door so I could get out and go home.

"Take care of yourself," he said.

"OK."

. . .

My dad waits on the porch until I climb the steps. It's late for him to be up, and I can tell he hasn't been to bed. He's still in his tin pants and boots. His sleeves are pushed up, and the front of his shirt is wet. He's holding the toilet plunger. It's easy enough to see what he had been doing before the trooper knocked. I open the door. Dad follows me in, shuts the door behind him, and turns off the porch light.

I could hear the trooper's car wheels on the gravel road. We always know when someone is coming or going to our place because you can hear the crunch of gravel. I like that sound.

When the sound of the trooper's car fades, I can hear the sound of the creek. It used to be a comfort, that sound, because that was what my world sounded like. It isn't a comfort anymore. I can hear my dad breathing. It is so quiet. But quiet doesn't last for long.

. . .

Dad didn't spend a lot of time making his point: "What the hell were you thinking? You weren't thinking. Just out cattin' around. You're useless as tits on a tomcat. What's the difference between you and her?"

What's the difference? Why am I not a dead girl? I don't for a minute know. I look at my dad. He can't let himself be sad. He can't let himself be frightened. But I've forced this moment. The fear jumps out of his eyes and into me like a hot spark.

"You could'a been the dead one."

That's when he hits me with the plunger, because I could have been the dead one. He hits me because it is easier to be angry than to be afraid. I could have been the dead one, but I'm not.

. . .

The coffee machine turns itself on, so the pot will be full of fresh, hot coffee when my dad comes down to leave for work. I kind of want to go hide in my room. I could pretend to be asleep. I don't go. Hiding isn't going to help. I'm ashamed of myself, and I can't hide from that.

It isn't like my dad is going to clobber me again. That's over. He isn't a violent man. If he wanted to kill me, he could have pulled the 30-06 off the rack and done it. If he wanted to cause me serious pain, he could have pushed me against the woodstove and left me with a burn to think about. He was just angry, and he had been trying to clear the toilet. He'd had enough crap to deal with, seriously. And then I show up in a cop car way after I should have been home.

He said I was as useless as "tits on a tomcat." I've heard him say that about a lot of mismanufactured, overpriced junk. He heard it plenty himself when he was growing up. It's almost like a family heirloom. I've said it myself. It was the first time he ever said it about me.

I would have rather been hit a few more times with the plunger.

. . .

The coffee was brewed at 5:30. Dad comes in the kitchen to get ready for work. It's way before light on Saturday morning, but Dad works whenever he gets the chance. He's lucky right now. Some guy's brother ripped off three fingers in a cable winch. So Dad has work—at least until some guy's brother is well enough to work hurt or the weather sours or the gyppo crew loses the equipment to the bank. Today there is work to be had, so he glops a couple of sandwiches together out of leftover stew and bread, pours the coffee in his thermos, and says, "You stay home today. I called your mom at work. She knows what happened. She told them you won't be making your shifts this weekend."

As soon as he's gone, I'm going to go outside and chop some wood. Fresh air and exercise. I need it. It's getting hard to keep my eyes open—and falling asleep at this point is a really bad idea.

. . .

Mom gets home from work a couple hours after Dad leaves.

I'm lying on the floor in the kitchen. I chopped wood until I lost control of the ax. Instead of biting into the chunk of dead tree, it bounced off and hit me flatside in the kneecap. For a minute, I didn't think of anything except how much it hurt. Then I realized it was time to stop.

Since then I've been curled up under the kitchen table. Waiting like a dog for my mom to come home.

I hear her tires on the gravel. I hear her steps on the porch. I hear the door open. I hear her changing her shoes—she is careful to keep the doughy white rubber clogs she wears at work clean and sanitary. She is going to feed the chickens now, just like she does every morning.

I follow her out and watch while she doles out kitchen scraps from an old metal pie pan. Stale bread, the ends of carrots, and soft spots cut out of potatoes—she drops the garbage out like treasures, and that is the way the chickens accept it.

Chickens don't always cluck, you know. When they are happy, they sort of hum—they chirp—they purr. The chickens are all around my mother waiting for her to make them happy. They are singing to her in their chicken way.

When I step closer, I can see my mom's back tighten up. She doesn't look at me. She watches the chickens.

I watch them too. I see how feathers ruffle in the wind. I see how Old Mean Gertie limps along without the ends of her toes. The chickens are very observant. Every scrap that drops is pecked up fast.

Mom says, "They were thinking of giving you a CNA shift at Cozy Pines. It wouldn't have been official, because you are underage and not certified, but we could have made it look like it was more hours in the kitchen. I could have taught you the ropes. We could have worked the same shift. . . ."

My mom flips the pie plate and slings the last of the garbage out. The sudden movement flusters the chickens– they scatter and stop singing.

"That isn't going to happen now," said my mom, "You missed the chance."

The wind shifts direction. It slaps me straight in the eyes. It smells like it might snow.

I missed the chance. If I had come right home last night, I could have started working night shifts with my mother at Cozy Pines. I could have just caught the bus from there in the morning, I guess, and everything else about school would have just stayed the same—except I don't know when I would have done my homework. Could I do calculus between emptying bedpans and tucking in sheets?

And maybe Esther would still be alive.

Because changing one thing, changes everything.

The chickens are getting calmer and are sideling clos-er to the scraps again. They have forgiven my mom for moving fast, but she hasn't forgiven me for being in the wrong place at the wrong time. I was undependable when she needed me to be dependable. I was sitting on a tailgate waiting to get drunk when I should have been ready to step into doughy white clogs and take up a bigger share of the load.

She still isn't looking at me.

But I'm looking at her. I can see the scar by the corner of her eye. She got it when she was learning to walk. She fell against a sharp corner on a coffee table. She made sure there were no sharp corners when I was little. When I was little, she used to call that scar her eye makeup. She used to say that when I was little. When I was little and she was happy.

"Get the eggs," Mom says, and she heads for the house.

. . .

There are seven eggs this morning. Most are already cold, but one is still warm from being inside the chicken-machine that turns carrot ends and earwigs into perfect shells and gobs of yellow yolk.

Eggs are beautiful. Their shape is ideal. The story about eggs is about how fragile they are, but they aren't, not always. It depends on how the pressure is applied. If you fling an egg out into the world like you're in the out-field and it's the ball, sometimes it bounces when it hits the ground. I have seen eggs bounce. Of course, I've seen eggs splatter too. That happens a lot more often.

Whenever they talk about the arrow of time, they use the example of an egg. "You can't unscramble an egg. Time flows in only one direction."

On a good day, I would try to understand the beauty of eggs and the puzzle of time. But it is not a good day.

My brain is itching.

. . .

*I need to go to school. I cook eggs. I eat the eggs. I get dressed. I walk to the bus stop.*

*The moon is full, and it's still up. It's a nickel in the western sky, round and shiny and not worth much. The snow catches the*

*moonlight and tosses it around until the world is three colors:*
*black, shadow, and snow light.*

*Trudge, trudge, trudge. Just keep walking down the wheel*
*ruts between the snow. It isn't far to the bus stop.*

*What is this? It looks like a little felt slipper. It is. It is a*
*little felt slipper. It is Asta's slipper. How could she have lost her*
*slipper? Where is she? Her foot will be cold without her slipper.*

*I want to call her, but I know she can't answer. She forgot*
*how to answer. How can she be lost here in the snow? Tracks,*
*there must be tracks. There are always tracks in the snow.*

· · ·

The moon is really there, but it isn't full, and there is no
snow. And there will be no slipper, because there is no Asta.

Asta is gone.

I know how to fight dreams, but I'm not sure I'm win-
ning. This time I woke up before The Bony Guy broke
my heart. He didn't get to hold out his web of bony fingers
and show me that he had Asta's other slipper. He didn't
make me scream in my sleep and wake up crying.

I'm awake, and I am not crying. I'm going to call it
a win.

## Chapter 3

# Applied Ballistics

Two hunters are arguing about whether a bullet rises or falls as it leaves the barrel. If the rifle is sighted horizontal to the surface of the earth, which hunter is correct? What forces are influencing the bullet's trajectory?

I thought maybe Dad and Little Harold would be around today. It's Sunday—even gyppos don't work on Sunday. They would have been a welcome distraction, even though Dad still isn't speaking to me directly, and I try to keep my distance from Little Harold when I'm bug-ass nuts. I mean, he's not even nine yet. He's entitled to some protection.

Maybe that's what Dad was thinking when he loaded the little guy into the truck this morning and left. Whatever the plan, I wasn't in on it.

. . .

They went to get a load of firewood, mostly. The back of the truck is pretty near full, but when Little Harold climbs down out of the truck, Dad reaches across the seat and hands him a bread sack. Dad points at me, on the porch, and Little Harold runs over holding the bundle out in front of him.

"Dad says we can have the liver right now. You'll cook it."

I take the plastic sack out of his hands. It's heavy. The wet contents slip around inside. Dad took a deer while he was out.

Back at the truck, Dad unties the blue tarp covering the load. There, on top, is one of Bambi's stupid brothers. We always call them Bambi's stupid brothers. It's a classic.

I stand by the sink and pull the liver out of the sack and rinse it off a little and drop it in a bowl of salt water to soak. There is a heart in the bag too. I take it out, hold it in my hand, rinse it off.

It doesn't look anything like what I saw on the highway. I stare at it: real heart. I shut my eyes: heart I imagined I saw. Not the same. This is real. The one I see with my eyes shut is not. It never was.

It never was.

I build up the fire in the cookstove and put the frying pan on to heat and chop up onions. I slice the liver into bits. It is perfect and healthy, no flukes, no sign of hunger or disease. If he hadn't made one tiny little error of trust today, Bambi's stupid brother would have probably lived through the winter. I drag the slices of meat through a pan full of flour and salt and pepper and drop them into the hot grease. Cook them quick and keep them tender. I brown the onions in the leftover fat and flour. Then I dish up a bowl for Little Harold and slide the rest onto a plate for my dad.

Let that be a lesson to you, Bambi's stupid brother. All it takes is one tiny miscalculation of trust.

. . .

I'm not better, but I am good enough to make it through the day. I have enough to keep me very busy. Too busy to sleep. Too busy to dream. I'd like to think I'm going to be too busy to see what isn't there, but I know better than that.

If you stay awake too long, you go crazy, they say. I say, what difference would it make? How much crazier can I get? I'll scrub the floors and the grout around the toilet and the oven to stay awake. Oven cleaner is better than smelling salts, you old-timey fainting ladies. Get with the program. Wake up and smell the methylene chloride.

So why not sleep and escape this crap? Good question. Sleep should be good, like being numb or being drunk, but it's not.

. . .

The problem with sleep is dreams.

I'm not the first person to say that. It gets said a lot, because it is true.

Most dreams are bad. This is a scientific fact. It isn't just me. I'm not special. Everybody's dreams suck. Some suck really hard.

I know way too much about dreams. I am an expert both in theory and practice.

The worst kind of dream is when you are just trying to shut your eyes and it's like a slide show. Eyes open: the real world. Eyes shut: you see what you don't want to see. The detail is amazing, but you can't look around and you can't look away. You shut your eyes, and there it is. It's like there is a camera that shows you the same bloody broken mess over and over again, frame by frame.

I'm standing at the kitchen table folding clothes. I know that. I can reach out and touch the wool socks. But what I know and what I see—not quite the same thing.

Eyes open: a little striped shirt in the laundry basket. Eyes closed: a lump of muscle that looks like a broken heart. Nothing new or weird about that. Been here. Seen that. The important thing to remember is that this is normal—for crazy people.

I even know its name: intrusive imagery. Esther's bloody heart isn't now, nor has it ever been, in the laundry basket. It's just a glitch in my brain. My programming is missing a breakpoint, and I'm stuck in an infinite loop. It's a processing problem, a stray spark lost in the dirty Jell-O inside my head.

. . .

There is nothing special about me. PTSD is common. They used to call it shell shock a hundred years ago almost. It happens to lots of people—guys who come back from the war, rape victims, little kids who lived through hurricanes—they all have to deal. *If* they can deal—otherwise, they lose it and end up like that crazy gray-haired Vietnam vet who lived in a culvert until he froze to death. Thinking about the images they see, the nightmares they have, it makes me feel like a coward.

I just need to focus on what is real—laundry to fold—and I need to remember those words *intrusive imagery.*

I may also need to be very aware of my breathing.

It's not a Zen thing. I have to breathe very carefully because intrusive imagery is only one of the sneaky traps I need to avoid. Memories can also hide in the smell of spilled diesel or hospital disinfectant. There is a proper name for that too. It's olfactory trigger: a smell that sets off a memory in your brain. Most people like them, I guess. Christmas tree needles or jasmine tea—somewhere people are probably seeking out those smells just so they can feel a wonderful memory light up in their imagination like twinkly lights. Me, not so much. I know that one unconscious breath can let a smell in and zap-zap-zap my brain will start sparking like a fork in a microwave.

Once that happens, I can blast my nose with garlic or Mountain Breeze air freshener or poisonous oven cleaner until tears run out of my eyes and I get a headache. It won't help. It takes more than another stink to fix that short circuit and avoid remembering.

And there is one other trap: dreams, plain-old-vanilla, recurrent-nightmare dreams. Living through everything once was bad, but not bad enough apparently, because it keeps happening again and again. My brain needs to understand what happened, so it gives itself another opportunity.

"Here," says my brain, "Let's just change this one thing. Changing one thing changes everything. You know that. Maybe if you have to ride to school in an ambulance. . . . Maybe if your little sister and your little brother are the same person. . . . Maybe if I make death into a recurrent character—call him The Bony Guy. See isn't that better now that you can see him? Just fiddle with the focus and make the picture sharper, sharp, sharp, sharper. Now he has a face—well, sort of a face. . . . Don't you feel better?"

My brain is not my friend.

. . .

When things are really bad, the best thing to do is to stay awake, and the best way to stay awake is to keep busy. So I stay awake until my eyes itch, I scrub the grout around the toilet with an old toothbrush, I make a pot of coffee, and I don't sit down. I go outside where the air is cold and I can hear the creek and see the stars. I chop wood. It's almost morning. I can tell by the position of the moon. Time to get Little Harold out of bed and give him some breakfast. I can hold on. I can get a handle on it.

Chapter 4

# The Veil Nebula

The luminous tendrils of the Veil Nebula are not the remnants of a dying star but are traces of the shock front that swept through space thousands of years ago after a supernova event. The energy released echoed outward, sweeping up dust and gas that fills the "empty" space between the stars. Compressed and charged with energy, the interstellar matter now emits its own light. If our perspective is edge-on, the shock front appears as a sharp filament. A face-on view presents the diffuse emissions or "veils" of light.

The minister who preached at my little sister's funeral screwed up her name.

The mistake is completely understandable.

We don't go to church. We just hired some guy to talk that day, I guess. Why would he have known?

It still gravels my dad, though. Sometimes I hear him saying under his breath, "Her name is Asta, Asta Sollilja. Not Ashley."

I thought of that at Esther's funeral.

Mostly, I try not to think about Asta. It'll never heal if you pick at it. That's what I think. But it was unavoidable today. There were too many memory triggers.

. . .

Esther's funeral was held in the same place as Asta's. I think the same dust was on the woodwork. The same air was in the room. Last winter we sat in a little, secret space near the front. We were very near the shiny, white box where Asta was hidden. It was just the four of us in that little space. Now Esther's family was sitting there, behind a sheer, dark curtain that kept them separate. The curtain hides them from prying eyes. It's a trick of light—or something about the angle of vision. I didn't know we were hidden when I was sitting there myself. It never occurred to me.

But now I'm outside. I understand that it has a purpose. The rest of the funeral audience can't see through that curtain. In that little room, you can have your grief in private, as long as you are quiet.

. . .

It surprises me to hear the minister at Esther's funeral say he didn't know her, since that family is religious. I wonder if they just picked his name out of the phone book. That's how we did it. Found a minister, I mean. I guess they are like gyppo loggers, just waiting for the chance to work.

However it happened, the guy talking today admits he didn't know Esther.

Then he launches into his stuff about how unprepared we are for someone so young to die. I give him some points for honesty, though not many. I felt like he was suggesting that it would have been easier if death was a scheduled event. Speaking from experience, sometimes we do expect someone young to die. Sometimes we have years of preparation. And it still hurts.

I give him some points for style. He tosses in a couple of nice metaphors, I notice. But he probably isn't sticking to the Bible as much as Esther's dad would like.

Esther's dad is a minister. His whole congregation is made up of his family. I haven't heard him preach, but he is known to be a strictly By-The-Book kind of guy.

It was impossible to know if he is angry with the pinch hitter at the pulpit. The sheer curtain—it really works. When you sit back there, you can see out. Things look a little gray, but you can see everything. From out here, nothing.

. . .

I wear the same dress for Esther's funeral that I wore when we buried Asta. The black wool sleeves are so tight I can't bend my arms. I shook it out before I put it on, but it still smells like the dust in my closet. The thread in the seams is stiff and pokes me up both sides and makes my armpits red and rashy. It fit better when I wore it that winter, but it was never comfortable.

It is a perfect dress for the job. It puts me in the right frame of mind, almost. It makes me uncomfortable enough that I look like I am sad.

. . .

Reba is here for the funeral too. She waves, but I don't wave back. I hope she figures out that it isn't personal. It's not like we are at the mall or something—waving at a funeral is just a little wonky.

Reba isn't wearing the right kind of clothes. She's got on a black dress too, but it's an LBD with sheer black sleeves and glittering beads that would attract magpies if she stood by the side of the highway.

Two things attract magpies: sparkly stuff and road-kill. This particular funeral is a jackpot for magpies. I can't share that with Reba.

A funeral is not a social event. A funeral is not a place for jokes.

Besides, my parents aren't letting me mingle and talk to anyone, much less Reba. The three of us just sit in the back row of chairs. We aren't close friends or family of the deceased. We are just here to pay our respects.

After the funeral, we don't go to the cemetery for the actual part, the part where there is a hole in the ground.

My parents and a bunch of other people who are paying their respects clump together in the parking lot of the funeral home.

"...the flowers—a little over the top. The florist probably gave them the hard sell. The kind of people who will take advantage of grief."

"...and it's terrible, just terrible."

"The driver is off the hook. It was a blind curve. He admitted he'd had a beer, but he wasn't going fast and the blood alcohol was way below the limit..."

"...just ran into the road in front of him."

Somebody had heard from somebody who knew somebody at the hospital who overheard that she was about eleven weeks pregnant.

"That family..."

"If she was pregnant, that'd explain it."

"Still, it's tragic, just tragic. And your heart goes out to that family..."

"That family..."

. . .

I don't like the thought that someone can go rummaging around in a body and tell all its secrets.

I know it happens.

I don't like to think about it.

I don't want to know if they did that to Asta.

All she had left was her little body.

Her little red hands with the scars where she chewed on them.

She didn't know they were her hands.

Or maybe she did.

Maybe it was just another sheer black curtain, and she could see out, but we couldn't see in so we didn't know she was there.

I want to believe she was gone way before the end.

I hope she was never really in the hospital. I hope she never felt the infection around the feeding port where we could squirt the food right into her stomach after she forgot how to swallow.

I hope when she mewed and mewed after we brought her home, it was just something her body was doing and it wasn't Asta.

I hope she wasn't scared or hurt when her heart stopped.

Please, please, please, it wasn't Asta anymore.

. . .

I saw Esther's family get into a big black car to go to the cemetery.

There were a lot of them. Her mother, her father. It was hard to tell which of them was the strong one and which one was blind with crying and ready to fall down. Then the kids like stairsteps: Faith, Abel, the missing step in the family where Esther used to be, Naomi, Ruth, Hope, and Gloria. There were even Faith's two kids: a toddler and a little blanket-wrapped bundle. There were enough to fill that big black car.

There weren't so many of us. The day of Asta's funeral, it was just Mom, Dad, Little Harold, and me in the shiny black car following the hearse. Little Harold was kind of big for it, but Mom pulled him onto her lap and cried in his hair. Little Harold was crying too. I think he was just upset that Mom was crying, but he might have been starting to understand what was happening. He was only seven then, but he's a smart kid, Little Harold.

. . .

Mom was pregnant with him when we started to lose Asta. We didn't know that then. She was disappearing from the inside out. We thought we were all good. When Little Harold was born, Asta was in the world. By the time he could talk, we knew she never would. His world has changed more than all of ours.

I think I might be the only one who can even think that Little Harold's world might have changed in a good way.

. . .

Asta was such a good baby. It wasn't just that she was pretty. Lots of little girls are pretty. She lived up to the name Dad found for her in a story he was reading—Asta Sollilja. It means "pretty sun lily."

She was a sunny baby. Complete strangers would stop what they were doing to watch her smile. As for me, I was desperately proud of her. She was my Asta too.

She didn't like her toys so much. That was all.

She was still warm and round, and I loved it when she would hold onto my thumb or finger.

I got to take care of her quite a bit after Little Harold was born. She was my living doll. I loved to dress her and fuss around with her hair. She never tried to get away from me. Now we know that might have been a sign, but we didn't know then.

Then one day, Mom took her along on a well-baby appointment for Little Harold. Little Harold was doing great, getting bigger and stronger every day. He was hitting every one of those "Your baby should be able to . . ." checkpoints.

For Asta, though, things looked a little different.

It is odd she stopped crawling.

Nothing big. Nothing to worry about yet.

It is odd she won't look the doctor in the eye.

Nothing big. Nothing to worry about yet.

It is odd she won't reach for the little flashlight.

Nothing to worry about yet.

Wait until the tests come back.

It is probably nothing.

Every baby has her own schedule.

What a pretty smile.

The doctor didn't even tell my mom what she was looking for when she ordered the tests. The doctor didn't tell my mom because she didn't want to find the little messed-up genes hiding in Asta's blood sample.

Doctors have to do a lot of things that are terrible.

## Chapter 5

# Evolutionary Developmental Biology (Evo-Devo)

A butterfly resting on a flower may seem far removed from the struggle for life described as nature "red of tooth and claw," but its existence began with the catastrophic destruction of another creature. A caterpillar is a functional organism. It eats, it moves of its own accord, and it has an interactive life. During the process of metamorphosis, the caterpillar is in fact demolished as the adult insect takes its place.

When the nightmares started, my parents said they would pass. Everyone has bad dreams. By April, though, my parents thought it might not be passing. My screaming in the night was making everybody edgy. So I started going to grief counseling at the clinic.

It was useful. The first day I went in, my mom made sure everyone was clear on the project. The insurance would pay for six visits. The plan was to get me fixed up in six hours or, if that wasn't quite possible, to make me stop screaming in the night.

. . .

The first visit I learned that there are some responses to grief that are pretty common: Denial, Anger, Bargaining, Depression, Acceptance.

It isn't like baking a cake where you follow the recipe and get it done:

1) Heat the oven to Denial
2) Prepare the pan with a spray of Anger
3) Mix in two medium-size Bargains with The Bony Guy
4) Add ⅓ cup of Depression (tears will do if you want low fat)
5) Bake for 35 minutes, or until you can jab a toothpick in your arm and it seems Acceptable.

It isn't a recipe. Some people only experience a couple of those things. It isn't a recipe, but it worries me.

The way I see it, we were in denial for years. The clock started when we got the diagnosis: Rett syndrome.

It's a genetic mutation.

If genes are the assembly manual for a person, there were pages missing from Asta's book. While she was a baby, we were still in the earliest pages, the first little modules were in place, and everything seemed fine. Then, when it was time to bring more of the assembled pieces together, some important pages were missing. Without those pages, things start to fall apart. She stopped trying to stand up. She stopped crawling.

The doctors told us what to expect: Her body will grow, but it will never be hers. She will not walk. She will not talk. She will always wear diapers. It may become harder and harder for her to swallow.

It doesn't matter. She is still our Asta. We know how to take care of our baby. And we are going to do whatever it takes as long as it takes.

And maybe science will catch up. If we can only hold on long enough, the missing pages might be found. And we can help her start over again.

But science didn't catch up.

. . .

After all those years of fighting hard, we lost. Now we get drunk. We hit each other. When the truck won't start, we punch the windshield so hard the shatterproof glass breaks. Is this depression or anger? Are we going to spend ten years or twenty doing this shit?

And what about bargaining? Did we just miss that part? Or maybe Mom and Dad were striking bargains all the time with The Bony Guy. Then, finally, they were all out of chips. Asta died. The Bony Guy always wins. He doesn't even cheat. Nothing up his sleeve but his radius, ulna, and humerus. Nothing funny about that, ba-dum-bump.

. . .

On the second visit to the grief clinic, I talked about a dream:

*I'm at the grade school and there is a dance in the room where we had rummage sales and showed movies and played dodgeball. The lights and windows have wire cages over them so when we throw balls at each other with lethal force we won't break any glass.*

*But we aren't playing dodgeball in the dream. It is a dance. Or maybe it is more of a cakewalk to raise money for the school. There is a circle of chairs, and they are all empty. The music starts and there are only two of us—just me and The Bony Guy dancing to the music.*

*It must be Halloween, because I am wearing a mask. So is The Bony Guy. He is a good dancer. He is a better dancer than I am and I'm going to lose the cakewalk. It is inevitable.*

*The music hasn't stopped, but I sneak out into the hall and then I push through the door into the playground. The moon is shining on the chains of the swings. I run across the road as fast as I can. The Bony Guy is smart and he will notice that I'm gone soon.*

*I cross a little creek. There is a board over it to make it easy. I could go to a house but I am sure The Bony Guy would know to look in there so I keep running. But then I see Asta. My dream-Asta is sitting by the water washing carrots. She looks like Little Red Riding Hood. I guess that is her Halloween costume. I try to tell her to run. The Bony Guy is coming. She has to run. Doesn't she see? She just keeps washing the carrots.*

*I give up and run away but I don't run far. There is a barn, a big old barn made out of squared logs with little tiny windows. There is a buffalo skull hanging over the door. I think it is hopeless to hide. The Bony Guy can find me if I hide. I need to keep running.*

*I know all that but I pull the door open and I try to hide in the barn. I find a window where I can watch Asta by the water. I see her. Then I blink, and she is gone.*

*The next time I blink The Bony Guy is standing beside me. I'm not scared. I'm just so tired.*

And when I woke up, I was still tired.

It isn't the sort of dream people have when they finally get to magic-happy-acceptance land.

. . .

My very favorite thing I learned during counseling happened during my fourth session.

I was talking about my dog, Ket. I don't know why. Maybe the clinic counselor liked dogs, and I saw a little flicker of happiness on her face when I mentioned mine. Counselors don't tell you much about themselves. That is part of the therapy bargain.

Ket was great. He used to sit by Asta and just let her crazy hands do whatever they had to do. Sometimes her hands would go bonk-bonk-bonk on the top of his head. Sometimes her hands would pull out some hair. That dog was always patient and let it happen. Ket was such a good dog.

On winter nights, Ket would manage to get us all in one corner of the living room. He would just kind of lean against your legs until you budged. He was so patient. First, he would budge one of us in the right direction, then another of us. When he was done, we would all be together. Asta would be in the middle, and we would all be together. Then Ket would sort of flop on the floor and grunt like it had been hard work but worth it.

"Border collie personality disorder!" the counselor giggled. "You have border collie personality disorder! God! Don't tell anyone I said that!"

I wouldn't have told, but it is true. I do have border collie personality disorder. I would like to get everyone into one corner where I could keep an eye on them and then I could take care of them.

I'm not proud of it. It is a mental disease.

. . .

I give the clinic counselors credit for doing what could be done. They let me know it wasn't the end of the world. They told me I could work through it. They gave me what I needed—like a sleep guard to protect my teeth so I didn't grind them into bits. They taught me how to watch

*43*

out for triggers—like the smell of Betadine. Then, when the six weeks were up, I said I was better. They did their best. I did mine. They said I should keep talking. They said that writing was also good, if I didn't have anyone to talk to. It didn't have to make sense, they told me. Just write like you are talking to someone who wants to listen. They told me to get lots of exercise. Finally, they offered me a prescription for antianxiety meds, but my mom said no to that.

I don't scream in the middle of the night.

I'm not sure that the clinic counselors would approve of my methods, but I don't scream in the night. I get exercise and I am writing, like they told me. But I do some other things too. When I have to, I stay awake all night and clean the bathroom grout.

And when I can get my hands on it, I drink. It sort of shuts things down, but it takes some care to reach the perfect level without getting sick. Then, when the depressing effects of the alcohol wear off, I wake up in the middle of the night, and it's almost impossible to get to sleep again. It isn't always easy to get anything to drink, so it is only an occasional solution. It's nothing I can rely on.

## Chapter 6

# Logical Problem Solving: Step-By-Step

1) Visualize and identify the problem. Make a sketch. Write a simple sentence that begins "I need to find out . . ."
2) Think about the problem FORMALLY.
3) Write equations that translate your "I need to find out . . ." sentence into mathematical terms.
4) Plug in the knowns and solve algebraically.
5) Check your work. Have you answered the question? Is the answer reasonable? Have you stated your answer properly (are units indicated, etc.)?

Preliminary thoughts on the Freak Observer:

I found a picture when I Googled "Freak Observer."

Visualization of the problem is the first step.

I learned that the very first day of physics. Step 1: "Visualize"

Everything has been simplified to a purple cereal bowl sitting on the table of time and space. Inside the big bowl are other, tinier bowls. Each little bowl is a universe.

In a little blue bowl, there is a tiny Earth. The little blue cereal bowl is our visible universe.

There are many little naked brains floating in the big purple bowl. They look like little tan walnuts, the brains do. Some are curled like chicks inside the shells of little bowls, but others are just "out there" in nothing. Those little brains floating all alone are the Freak Observers.

Their job is to observe what we do not.

It must be frightening for the Freak Observer. It just pops into existence because it is hard for nature to make a whole universe. It is easier to create bits and pieces—a boot, a planet, a naked brain floating around in nothingness. It's just there, and it is conscious, so it observes and it remembers and it tries so hard to understand.

. . .

I wonder if Mr. Banacek thought much about Freak Observers before he wrote down the words and put the slip of paper in the extra-credit jar.

Honestly, this is not an ordinary physics problem.

"I need to find out . . ." I have no idea how to finish that sentence.

I wonder what Mr. Banacek thinks the right answer is.

Wondering what other people think is a dead end.

Even if they tell you, you can never be sure.

Especially, maybe, if they tell you.

Lies happen.

. . .

"Take care, Loa," says the bus driver.

I swear, if I hear that shit one more time, I will not be responsible for my actions.

I know how to take care.

I can wash dishes, pull out slivers, sharpen a chainsaw, thaw out frozen pipes, pack a lunch, mop floors, serve five hot plates to a table, get poop stains out of little boy's underwear, and sterilize a nasogastric tube.

What do you want me to take care of?

Shall I stop the glaciers from melting?

How about malaria? For, like fifty cents, I can keep a family in Africa from dying of malaria.

If I get knocked around with a toilet plunger, does that mean somebody else doesn't? OK. It's a deal. I'm your girl.

I'll take care of it.

. . .

I trip up the stairs on the way to first period.

My stuff flies out of my bag and ricochets up, down, and sideway. Pens, calculator, idiotic index cards required for English: Kablooee! The stairs are crowded between classes. There I am, on my hands and knees. Nobody stops. Nobody bumps into me. Nobody even laughs. Nobody steps on my stuff. Nobody steps on my hands as I grab for my stuff and try to put things back in the bag.

I'm not invisible.

People just don't want to look at me.

A couple of my teachers won't call on me.

People don't want to see me anymore.

I used to be Corey's friend, and that was cool, but now I'm that dead girl's friend, and that is not cool. People used to smile and say, "Hey!" but now I'm like a pile of guts on the highway. Sure they see me, but they have places to go, and it would be weird and sick to stop and say, "What's up?"

. . .

Mr. Banacek brought an orrery to physics class this morning. It's like a clockwork model of the solar system. There are little metal spheres on little wire arms, and when you turn a little knob, the spheres travel through orbits. It's a gear-driven wonder that almost works most of the time. It needs a little push now and then to keep the solar system moving.

I love it.

It's pure beauty.

. . .

Mr. Banacek collects stuff about space.

He told us about himself the first day of class.

When he was a kid, he watched Apollo rocket launches on TV—and *Star Trek*. He told us about how the stuff on *Star Trek* was so futuristic for the time, like automatic doors. They had to have some guy pull the doors out of the way when they made the show. Now the doors at the grocery store slide back just like the ones in *Star Trek* but for real. And those weird little communicators? They made them out of saltshakers. There was no such thing as a cell phone.

We are living in the future. Except space travel didn't really work out, and the closest thing to an alien is the almost invisible traces that might be a fossil of a bacteria found on a meteorite in Antarctica.

The future: not quite as advertised.

So now Mr. Banacek has an antique orrery and a scraggly gray ponytail and teaches high school physics. He may also get dressed like a Klingon and pretend to eat worms while he watches the Sci-Fi channel. He didn't confess to anything like that, though.

He brought in his scrapbooks about the Apollo missions that first day. He started them when he was a kid. There are no cute coordinating papers or stickers, just page after page of newspaper clippings and pictures torn out of magazines stuck in place with yellow tape. I flipped one open, and there was The Bony Guy.

It was a political cartoon. The Bony Guy was standing by a smoking rocket. He was wearing a space suit and was holding the helmet under his arm. He was grinning, because The Bony Guy is always grinning.

"Did you forget me?" asked The Bony Guy, "I've been on every trip."

Mr. Banacek saw me looking at the page.

He told me three Apollo astronauts died, burned during a test on the launchpad. They were going to the moon. They burned up instead.

"I thought about that," he said, pointing at The Bony Guy. "I thought about that cartoon when we lost the shuttles—*Challenger* and *Columbia*. And I realized it would never stop us. Fear is not enough to stop us."

Then he made the conversation bigger, turned it into a mini-lecture to the class.

Another Apollo mission, 13, almost failed, but the astronauts were able to save themselves. They knew the math, so they figured out the way home. And they had duct tape, so they could make some creative repairs.

The class perked up its ears at the mention of duct tape. Everyone understands duct tape. Shit, you can earn a scholarship by making a prom dress out of duct tape. Most of our lives are stuck together with duct tape. Rip your jeans? Duct tape to the rescue. Want to commit a crime? Bring duct tape. You can use it to tie people up—and muffle their screams. Gash your leg with an ax? Use duct tape for a heavy-duty bandage.

Astronauts used duct tape to fix the moon buggy too. They patched that sucker up just like it was a beater car.

Once upon a time, Mr. Banacek wanted to go to the moon. Now he's in a classroom trying to get us to remember things that happened before we were born. He wants us to be amazed by duct tape and ingenuity. Or maybe he just wants to remember when he was amazed.

Chapter 7

# Orbital Physics

A mysterious corporation wants to place a satellite in geostationary orbit over a specific equatorial island. Can you tell the corporation what the angular velocity must be to achieve its evil, evil goal?

My family used to work like an orrery. We would have got a prize in a science fair, our gears turned so smoothly and all the parts fit together so perfectly. Asta was in the middle, where the sun ought to be. The rest of us kept to our orbits. We never crashed into each other. No one ever went missing like a rogue comet.

My orbit went like this: get up, check Asta's diaper, take a shower, eat my breakfast, get dressed, walk to the bus, be at school, come home, cook dinner, get Little Harold in a bath, get him in his PJs, listen to Dad read to Asta while I do the dishes, do my homework, go to bed.

Dad's orbit involved work at the mill, fixing things (something always needs fixing), and reading.

He sat by Asta and read aloud to her every night. He started his reading project right after he dropped out of high school. He liked to read, but he decided he didn't want to waste his time, so he started reading Nobel Prize winners. He figured that would weed out the crap. Dad is very direct that way. He doesn't reinvent the wheel.

Asta probably didn't understand the stories he read to her about a black sorrel mare on the flower-strewn avenues or farting Chinese buses. But maybe she heard her name when he read about stubborn people in Iceland. Maybe the sound of her name meant something to her. Or maybe it meant no more than other names from other stories. Eréndira. Umaima. If Dad had opened a different book during the nights before Asta was born, she might have had a different name. Just like if I had been a boy, I would have been Harold. But I'm Loa because Mom liked the sound. Asta might have had a different name, but she still would have been slipping away from us.

But when Dad read at night, she stopped grinding her teeth and swallowing air.

When Dad read, we all grew still, and we were all together.

Even Little Harold's speedy orbit slowed down enough for sleep to take over. It wasn't like he was listening, but he knew he was supposed to be a little bit quiet, to stop running and bouncing off the walls.

My little brother basically operates at two speeds: sonic fast and sound asleep. He hits the floor running every day with big plans and exciting ideas. Usually he starts talking in the middle of a sentence when he wakes up. I don't know if it was half said when he fell asleep or if he's finishing a conversation he was having in his dreams. Little Harold talks to himself a lot, because no one else has a clue what he is talking about most of the time.

One day I caught him dyeing field mice green with food coloring. He'd made himself a live trap out of a bucket. It was pretty nifty engineering for a little kid. Anyway, he was involved in some sort of experiment that required the mice to be green, but I made him turn them loose. The other day, he was talking about a fire-type Pokémon in our woodshed, which worries me when

I think about it—Pokémon may be imaginary, but fire isn't, and the woodshed would burn like crazy if Little Harold started a fire in there.

Still, show me any kid in footie pajamas who trots in a perfect elliptical orbit day after day and I'll show you a screwed-up kid. Little Harold was doing just fine. He was doing just what a kid ought to do.

Mom's orbit was like the orbit of moms through time. The features of her days were mostly food, messes, and worry. Cave women had days like that, with the occasional cave bear added to the mix. Homesteading women had days like that, with blizzards and plagues of locusts to break the monotony.

My mom's orbit passed through a lot of clinic waiting rooms and emergency room visits while she was taking care of Asta. I think she would have been glad to swap that for a cave bear or a plague of locusts. Those are temporary challenges. A person can at least put up a fight against a cave bear, maybe win with a long enough stick and a sharp enough rock. A person can hunker down and wait out a cloud of locusts—cut the horse loose from the buckboard, hide the baby under your skirt, and grit your teeth while the bugs crawl all over you. It isn't fun, but it's doable. It's doable because maybe you won't have to bury that baby. Maybe the bear won't eat it. But there is no way to fight a genetic defect—I know that now. Mom probably knew it a long time ago, but she never stopped orbiting. She always kept her face turned toward Asta.

So that was how we spent our lives. We were a shiny bright machine, a family of planets circling our own little star.

And then The Bony Guy took a sledgehammer to us.

. . .

I wonder why they sent an ambulance the night Asta died. It wasn't like there was any hurry anymore. They didn't turn on the siren or lights when they came or when they went. The only sound was the crunch of the tires on the gravel. Silent ambulances give me the creeps.

Maybe they sent it because bodies fit in ambulances. The paramedics have the wheeled carts that slide right in. Everything was convenient.

At the point the ambulance and paramedics came, I was glad to have something to think about. I was sitting in my grandfather's chair by the window holding Little Harold on my lap. I was supposed to take care of him, to keep him out of the way. He didn't really need to see anything. He wouldn't understand what was going on, and Mom and Dad needed to think about Asta and the arrangements. He would have probably liked to watch some cartoons, but that just seemed wrong. So I held him and asked him questions about Pokémon. He always had a lot to say about Pokémon.

Once in a while, I would say something like, "I like Cubone."

That would get him revved up again, "The lonely Pokémon. Did you know that skull on his head belonged to his mom? He isn't very strong. Even when Cubones revolve—"

"Evolve."

"Eee-volve . . . evolve into Marowak, they aren't so powerful. I like Pikachu and Mew and Hypno and Chimchar. They are a way lot stronger. Chimchar has a fire on his tail."

I needed something to think about while he was talking, and so I focused on the ambulance. After it finally left, after I couldn't hear the tires crunching on the gravel anymore, Dad came in and said we should all try to get some sleep.

So I took Little Harold into his room and put him under his covers. Then I told him to budge over, and I climbed in with him. Usually, I hate it if I have to share a bed with Little Harold. He's got sharp little elbows and kicks off the covers. That night, though, I wanted to hold him. I waited until he fell asleep before I let myself cry. Tears are kind of oily, have you noticed? I hate the wet spot they make on the pillow, but I couldn't turn it over without waking Little Harold.

I was just there in the dark, listening to Little Harold breathe, wishing I could go to sleep.

I never wish for sleep anymore.

· · ·

*We are on Mars, I think, because the world outside is full of red dust blowing through the air. I shut the curtains because I don't want to see that red dust. It looks like powdered blood. It's just so dismal.*

*I'm trying to put an orrery together, but I can't find the ball that is supposed to be the sun. I think it might have rolled under the bed.*

*Then I realize that the real sun has disappeared—not just gone down, disappeared. This planet and all the other planets are going to stop going around in circles. Everything is perfectly dark. The planets are flying blind. I can feel heat leaking out of my body.*

*I can hear someone breathing. It isn't me. Then I see The Bony Guy. He is giving off his own light, like a glow stick. He is holding the ball from the orrery. He is holding the sun, and he isn't going to give it back.*

## Chapter 8

# Collision of Elastic Bodies

Two elastic bodies collide. Body One has a velocity of 4 m/s. Body Two is at rest. Find their velocities after collision. Would this result be observable on a pool table?

The ride to school is a little better since there is less gawking when we go past the blind curve where Esther died. The exploded tree is still there. The black-on-black skid marks on the pavement are still there. Eventually, I guess there will be one of those little white crosses to remind people that death is around every corner, in every barrow pit, and at every intersection, but there isn't one yet. Looking out the window when we pass just isn't the most interesting thing to do anymore. It's yesterday's gruesome. Nothing to see here, folks.

I still try to focus on something else when we go by that place. Like the boot on the jerk across the aisle. It's got shit on it. He could have knocked it off, but he's a jerk, so he didn't, and now he's got his feet up on the seat. I don't want to get all Miss Manners, but what a fuckwad.

The fuckwad's boot. I need to keep my mind on the fuckwad's boot. For one thing, it's a lot better than noticing that he keeps sticking his hand down his pants and scratching his unit. For another, I don't want to go where my mind might take me if I looked out the window.

The fuckwad's boot. The theory of the Freak Observer has something to say to the fuckwad's boot.

It says, "It is easier to create a boot than a universe. It is easier to create a naked brain than to a create whole creature. And everything is so infinite that those things are bound to happen—Boot!—Brain! Do you understand?"

The boot says nothing. A chunk of shit falls off it, but it says nothing.

It is now safe for the brain to look out the window.

. . .

That Friday that Esther died, I was standing outside, waiting for the bus when she yelled out the truck window and asked if I wanted to ride home with her and Abel.

I wonder, if I had ridden the bus like I was supposed to, would I be working the graveyard shift with Mom at Cozy Pines? Would Esther still be dead?

It doesn't matter if the answer is yes or no. This is not a thought experiment. She can't be alive and dead at the same time like Schrödinger's imaginary cat. Esther is dead—and I know it.

. . .

If you are in a hurry, a school bus is the worst possible travel option. It moves slowly down its route, stopping at trailer parks, gravel roads, private drives, and railroad tracks. It doesn't matter if there is no train. A bus stops and flaps its doors. It doesn't matter if there is no one waiting to go to school. The bus stops and flaps its doors.

One day while I was riding the school bus, I made a rough estimate of all the time I've spent being hauled around. It made me sad, that number. Should I count the time waiting for the school bus in the dark? Should I count the time spent walking through the snow to get to the bus stop?

It's not like I have any place better to be.

Mostly, I read while I'm on the bus. If you need proof that I have no friends, you have it now: I read on the bus. Sometimes I try to write, even though it's impossible to write without scribbling and making a mess. When I don't have a book, I just stare out the window at things I have seen so many times before. We are at the animal shelter corner. We turn north. We pass the university, and then we go over the bridge. We take the ramp onto the interstate and zoom through the canyon, past the truck stops and trailer courts with no interstate access. You can't get there from here or here from there. We lose the interstate, and we are on the two-lane winding road that follows the river. Here is the lumber mill where my dad used to work. Here is the curve where Esther died. Here is another bridge, the river winds around, and another bridge. And here is the road home. All I have to do is get out, cross the railroad tracks, go up the hill, through another trailer court, past the cliff, past a place that frightens me in my dreams, up a hill, through a barbwire fence, down a hill, and I'm home. Yahoo!

Home. It's overrated.

. . .

My dad is very big on Home. He grew up in this house. When he was born here, they had electricity, but no running water. A flush toilet is a very big deal when you compare it to an outhouse. No more going out in the cold and the dark. No more being afraid that a bear will eat you while you are out there. No more being afraid that you might fall in the hole, which is a serious fear when your butt is so much smaller than the hole. No more using a stick to break the poopsicles that grow up and up in the winter. When they got a toilet, he ran outside after he flushed. He ran as fast as he could to the big hole in the backyard.

"Bye-bye, turdie!" he would yell when the water poured into the hole.

He was kind of sad when they put railroad ties and dirt over the top of the cesspit and covered it up. It wasn't the same—waving when he flushed. It was sort of a nonevent.

That's progress. Disappointing.

My dad used to tell me lots of stories about when he was a kid. Now he doesn't. He hardly talks at all. We walk past each other like ghosts. Sometimes I wonder if I died when Asta died, but I didn't notice.

. . .

If I am a ghost, then I chose a strange house to haunt. There are no mysterious cold places that can't be explained by lack of insulation. There are no rustling sounds in the middle of the night that aren't caused by mice or squirrels or bats in the eaves. When doors swing open, it's because they don't fit in the doorjambs and the house is settling. I don't have a nifty EMF meter or other gadgets like the ghost hunters on TV have, but I think the readings would be inconclusive at best. If those ghost-hunter guys came, they would be pretty disappointed, but that doesn't mean we aren't troubled by the dead.

The thing about ghosts is that they haunt your head. My dad can't pour a cup of coffee without remembering his mother—she used the same blue enamel mug for her own coffee. My grandfather used to sit in that chair by the window, so we leave that chair by the window. It's been more than a year, but Mom still has to remind herself not to buy diapers for Asta when she goes to town.

Ghosts are mostly habits of memory. In an old house like this, everything you touch is connected to another moment. The cupboard is full of ghosts. The bookmarks between pages are ghosts. The photographs of my unattractive ancestors on the wall are most certainly ghosts. Even the morning glories that grow by the back porch are ghosts. My mom plants them every year. She soaks the little black seeds and nicks them with a nail file so they will be able to crack open and grow. She plants them because there were morning glories blooming the day she came to the house.

. . .

It could almost pass as some great romance, if my parents weren't involved.

My mom landed in Montana by accident. She was in a car full of people who had pooled their food and gas money and were going to Seattle on a road trip. She got sick of them, or they got sick of her. The car pulled away, and she was standing there with a blue nylon backpack that held everything she owned in the world. They didn't leave her any of the collective food and gas money, but they did give her a lovely parting gift, a joint of not really good weed. She smoked it. It didn't change things much. It wasn't very good stuff.

When a truck came by, she stuck her thumb out. It was my dad. He was wearing a red plaid shirt, and he smelled like sweat and chainsaw fuel. They were both alone. She either didn't have a home or didn't want to go back there. He had a home and a job and didn't want to wake up in fifty years to find himself sitting on the edge of a single bed in pee-stained underwear. Like I said, some great romance.

Once I found a little stationery box on a shelf in a closet. On the outside, there was a pink My Little Pony with silvery wings and silver stars on its butt. Inside the box, there were some pieces of paper. They were probably letters, but I couldn't read cursive yet. There was a birthday card with a picture of a wiener dog eating the frosting off a cake. There were some photos too. An old black-and-white one of some people standing in a street by a car. A color snapshot of a boy, but someone had cut his face out of the picture so all there was left was a round hole. I stuck my finger through the hole and was wiggling it around. When Mom found me with the paper and photos all scattered on the floor, she was not happy. She took the box and the rest of it away, and I have never seen any of it again.

Wherever that box is, it is all that is left of my mom's life before Dad.

Most of the stuff in this house belonged to my ghost grandparents. The kitchen stove, the teakettle, the frying pan, the table and chairs. It isn't like they are precious heirlooms. They are beat-up pieces of junk, but they work. Until something is broken beyond repair, my dad doesn't see the point in making any kind of change.

That, right there, could be the formula of my parents' mysterious romance: random motion + the inertia of rest = True Love.

. . .

Fate has a mean streak. A girl gets in a car full of less-than-perfect strangers, crosses the mighty Mississippi, drives through the night past places where wagon trains stopped to bury people killed by fevers and stupid mistakes. She makes it past the first pile of mountains and, for no really good reason, decides she doesn't want to go to Seattle after all. She sticks out her thumb. A lonely guy in a pickup pulls over. She climbs in. Then, all of a sudden, two rotten, cracked little bits of DNA are just that close to each other. Two rotten, cracked little bits of DNA waiting for their chance.

I was lucky. Asta wasn't.

## Chapter 9

# The Sum of All Forces in a System Equals Zero

Give an example of each:
1) Stable equilibrium
2) Unstable equilibrium
3) Neutral equilibrium

There was this little window of time after Asta died when things were going to be OK. Things were different, but it wasn't all bad. I went to grief counseling at the clinic. I had more free time after school.

Things weren't perfect. Dad stopped reading at night. Mom and Dad argued about how to get rid of the equipment we didn't need anymore like the wheelchair and the hospital crib. Sell it, throw it in the dump, keep it forever, give it away—I don't even know what they decided to do. I wasn't part of the conversation.

I was having this exciting new life as a normal person. Or trying to. I wasn't off to a flying start.

To be honest, I stumbled before I got started. I'm kind of bad at normal.

There were a couple of things holding me back. First, I wasn't exactly sure what kind of normal I wanted to be.

I could try to be normal like the other kids who ride Bus 32 are normal. I could just join the herd. It wouldn't be hard to blend in. I know the local customs. After all, I had years to learn them. I had been 33.33 percent of my class for nine years, counting kindergarten. Reba and Esther were the other 66.66 percent. But now I was a little less than 0.5 percent of my freshman class. It wasn't like the good old days in grade school where there was only one toilet and if the seat was warm when you sat down, it was a sure thing that you knew the name of the person whose rump warmed it up.

Nope. It was a big school. There were a lot of toilets and many ways of life to choose.

Reba, for example, chose a tech-ed track.

This was only partly because she likes to be around guys and there are a lot of guys who do tech-ed. Boys are not Reba's first love. Driving is her first love. She learned to drive while bumping around a field in an old truck when she was so little that she had to hang onto the steering wheel like a kitten while she stretched to reach the pedals with her tiptoes. The damn truck always stalled when she had to shift gears. I know this because she took me for rides when I spent the night at her house. She tried to teach me how to be her gear shifter, but I was hopeless. I picked up a lot of new vocabulary from Reba—the kind of words that are useful when dealing with trucks that stall and friends that can't shift gears.

She still likes driving as much as she did when she was five, and she has a talent for understanding engines. The summer after she graduates, she is going to Pit Crew U. Her mom has promised. Reba wants to be on a NASCAR pit crew, and you don't get there from here by wishing. That's why she is still riding the bus with the rest of us mouth breathers instead of driving herself to school. She and her mom are saving up so she can go to Pit Crew U, and every buck they don't spend on gas matters.

Reba had her life figured out at fourteen.

A part of me envies that.

I sure don't have life figured out.

On the other hand, nobody's figuring my life out for me, either.

Esther's life was figured out for her.

She didn't have any more to say about it than a heifer.

I feel ashamed for saying that.

It makes her seem lumpy and stupid. She wasn't. Her future just wasn't up to her.

To be honest, maybe nobody gets to pick their future. But her situation was a little more intense.

The list of subjects she couldn't learn about in school was pretty long. All books have to be preapproved by her father. He doesn't approve of much. Most of the time, the teacher has to come up with a suitable substitute. History books that cover anything "pre-Biblical" are forbidden, because there isn't anything pre-Biblical. Dinosaurs are OK as long you assume they could have strolled into town and helped build the pyramids. Health classes when the teacher does sex ed are not allowed. This includes dopey little booklets about your period and sample tampons.

Esther could take whatever math classes she wanted. Unfortunately, she wasn't especially good at math and she had no love for it.

All these rules meant Esther was going to be sitting in the hall or the office most of the time while "forbidden" subjects were covered in the core classes.

She could always take Family and Consumer Science. She could make chili or biscuits or macaroni and cheese in Culinary Arts. She could set the table and wash dishes and iron shirts—just like at home. She could take Textiles and Apparel as long as the teacher provided patterns for "modest" sewing projects. She could be busy and productive, churning out casseroles and pot holders like a maniac, as long as the teacher never mentioned anything that could be dangerous to her moral values, like women working outside the home.

To be fair, though, Esther never complained about her life—ever. In all the years I knew her, she never complained.

Then there was me. I have no idea what I want to do, not really. And nobody was making my choices for me. So when we had to register for classes, I signed up for all the classes I thought sounded like things people who go to a university need to know. People who go to a university don't make pot holders or rebuild transmissions—that's what I figured. They can speak French and program computers and do science in a laboratory—that's what I figured. Nobody told me any different.

So I just swam through the crowds in the halls to my classes. I did my homework. I got good enough grades. When I wasn't thinking about an experiment or a test question, I was thinking about what I had to do when I got home. I planned what to make for dinner, and I worried if I remembered to start the load of laundry for Mom before I left that morning.

I have a tendency to frown and chew on my lower lip when I plan and worry. I didn't know that then. It turns out that I was making major decisions about my social life without really trying. I found my personal way-to-be:

I was a scowling–anti-social–geek–girl. As it turns out, this was not a good place to start on my journey to normal.

…

Even scowling anti-social geeks aren't immune to the power of friendship. Friendship is for everybody.

That sounds uplifting, like a "very special" episode of a stupid sitcom. Friendship! Friendship is for everybody! But exposure to friendship is pretty much an accident of time and place. And the power involved is high-voltage—lightning-bolt scale. When friendship moves through you, it leaves a mark.

All friendships are unequal. If they weren't, power couldn't get swapped back and forth. We would just hover in our self-contained envelopes producing everything we need and eating our own shit. "Mmmmm!" we would say, "That's good shit." And we would all be perfectly happy and immortal, like yeast.

Imagining a friendship between equals is sort of like imagining angels dancing on a pin. Does it matter if they are raving or pirouetting? What's the point, really, other than the one on the other end of the pin?

I am not a happy little yeast or floaty little angel. I am a bad friend.

When it comes to the power of friendship, I am a black hole. Fun, money, creativity—whatever—I'll just swallow it up. Eventually, I will collapse, and when I do, I'm going to take you with me. Consider yourself warned.

## Chapter 10

# A Philosophical Zombie

A philosophical zombie (p-zombie) is indistinguishable from a normal human being except that it lacks conscious experience. If you kick a p-zombie, it will behave as if it felt pain, but it does not have the experience of pain. If you were such a zombie, you wouldn't know it (because you would lack consciousness) and neither would your friends (because, if they asked, you would insist that you were a normal human being).

I had a friend, once.

I probably shouldn't be so dramatic. That sort of thing can be irritating. Still, there is some truth to the drama.

I've known a lot of people, grown up with people, and done stuff with people. I know what color their bedrooms are and if they like to eat a dill pickle before they go to sleep. I watched people outgrow sweatshirts. I've played No Bears Are Out Tonight in the mountains at night, while I was drunk, and there probably really were bears, but there were certainly warm bodies and excitement and hiding in the dark.

But friendship is something more than breathing the same air or touching the same basketball. Not much more, maybe, but something. I speak from experience here. Like I said: I had a friend for a while.

It was after Asta died. I'm not sure why it happened. Maybe Mrs. Bishop sicced him on me and told him to fetch me in like a bummer lamb. Or maybe grief is like magnetism—some it repels and others it attracts. Whatever the reason, it didn't last forever. I am a bad friend. That's part of the explanation. But I think maybe my friend was even worse. Like I said, friendship leaves a mark.

. . .

Teriyaki chicken, rice pilaf, stir-fry vegetables, mandarin oranges, and cinnamon roll. I like to eat school lunch. Seriously. I like to eat what I don't have to cook. Yay! for canned mandarin oranges. Yippy! for vegetables that look different but taste, oddly, the same. I even enjoy eating with a fork I don't have to wash. I was sitting there enjoying the finer things in life when someone actually made a point of sitting down across the table from me.

I recognized him from French class: Some guy called *Guy*.

Then he stuck his finger into the goo on my cinnamon roll. Then he smiled.

"Hi, Loa," he said, "Want to be my debate partner?"

"Want to keep your hands out of my food?"

"Now that, right there, is one of the reasons why you and I should be debate partners. You ask the tough questions. I set you up to ask them, and you ask them." Then he stuck his finger in his mouth and sucked off the frosting. He made that frosting look better than it was. That frosting looked great.

"Really. I've watched you," he said. "You're smart and you're mean. We can start practicing after school today. You'd enjoy it. I know you would, eviscerating some poor guy from Two Dot, Outer-East-Montanagolia, who couldn't find Africa with both hands if it was tattooed on his ass. Think about it. A world of wonder awaits."

"I ride the bus. My mom . . . "

"Call your mom. Moms like this kind of shit."

"I don't have a phone."

"I have a phone. Call her." He slid a pretty piece of machinery across the table.

"Tell her you can spend the night with Corey. Tell her she doesn't have to drive into town or anything. You'll bring home the permission slips tomorrow."

So I did. And it worked.

I handed the phone back.

"Who is Corey?" I asked. "And do you have permission to invite people to spend the night at her house?"

"Way to insult your new best friend," he said. "Let me introduce myself, I'm Corey." He raised his hands, palms up and arms wide, ready to be adored. He only held the pose for a moment, just long enough to make sure I, his audience of one, was with him. This is Corey. His hair is the color of a red-haired bear, a cinnamon bear, and nobody's hair looks that good and that messed up unless it's a plan. He wears a plain white T-shirt because he doesn't need to send any messages to anyone about anything. His mouth is sort of small, and he doesn't grin, but the corners are always turned up the way a dolphin always seems to be smiling. But it's a bad idea to assume that dolphins are happy—that's just the shape of a dolphin mouth. And this is just the shape of Corey's.

"AKA *Guy*."

"*Et votre nom est Lulu?*" He shook his head like it was amusing somehow that I was still tugging on the leash.

"I get your point."

. . .

I saw deep scratches in the side of the little car. Not the kind left behind by a steering miscalculation, the kind that happen when someone drags a key or a screwdriver across the paint.

"I am not universally loved," he said as he unlocked the door to his Mini Cooper. He fidgeted with his phone, "Manu Chao? Wimme? Drive-By Truckers? What random delights shall we hear?"

There were some big-ass speakers in that itty-bitty car. Where? I do not know—under the drift of Chinese food cartons and crumpled-up sweaters and the abandoned pages of homework with muddy footprints on them, maybe. Wherever they were, they were good enough not to buzz even though the sound getting pushed through them was dramatic. Visceral even, as in I could feel it pushing the molecules around in my kidneys and lungs.

The song was unfamiliar: There is a girl jumping off the stairs and somebody promises to catch her, but they don't. Later, she feels guilty.

In a few weeks, I would know all the words.

But that day, I just listened. I just watched Corey and wondered how he could stay on the road while he threw his head back, shut his eyes, beat the rhythm on the steering wheel, and howled out the lyrics.

. . .

Their garage was bigger than our barn. We don't have a garage, so there isn't anything but the barn to compare with this place.

A garage door slides open before the Mini stops in front of it.

"Welcomed home with open arms, right house?" says Corey.

"Mom enjoys convenience, so the garage door is programmed to recognize our cars and 'Open, *mes amis.*'"

Inside the garage, there are two other rigs, a Ram Club Cab truck and a Prius. The garage is like a scene in a cartoon about cars who are very different but learn that they are not so different after all. Then they have a happy ending.

But, really, these cars *are* so different—and they hate each other. Secretly, the Prius is waiting for the day when gas runs out and she gets to laugh manically while the Ram truck suffers. The Ram likes to crowd into the Mini's space and scare him so much he leaks oil.

Corey interrupts my scowling examination of the cars.

"It depends on who Mom needs to impress. Some of her clients are Ram truck people. Some are Prius people. Today she must not be working because she is driving her Volvo. It's her midlife crisis car. Volvo, vulva, whatever. It makes her happy."

I follow Corey like a stray dog through the house, which is all beautifully lit and new and enormous. Basically, it is all just not-like home.

I'm staring at the little stream—no shit, a babbling brook—that runs through a corner of the dining room. There are big white and red goldfish swimming around in there.

"Mom thinks aquariums and fountains are not very imaginative," says Corey, and he hands me a glass of water.

But it isn't water. It smells like ripe pears and shines more purely than mountain spring water. This I know for a fact, because we have a mountain spring at home. Spring water does not smell like pears. We have a stream at home too, but it's behind the house, not in it. There are little rainbow trout in our water, not goldfish.

"Wodka," says Corey.

"Thanks." The vodka is delicious.

A little round robot vacuum cleaner peeks into the dining room, thinks better of it, and backs away.

"Mom has it programmed to start as soon as I come home. She thinks I leave a trail of crumbs behind me so I can find my way back to the bathroom." Then he points at the shy little robot pacing in nervous rows in the other room.

"The first one fell in the creek. It turns out they are not intended for vacuuming koi. Koi don't do so good when they have a run-in with a robot either."

Then we went downstairs through the home gym and into the game room.

. . .

Corey and I spent a lot of time stretched out on the pool table in his basement in the dark. It is a surprisingly comfortable place to be. There are no windows. When he switches the lights off, it is totally dark. It's so dark, my eyes start to make up moving splotches of blue light and I get a little dizzy.

If I paid attention, I could feel the warmth of his body even though we weren't touching. We were stretched out head to foot on a pool table in the dark. We were not touching. I could hear his breathing, and I could almost feel the beating of his heart. Or was that some echo of my own heart? I didn't care. I was warm and safe and full of vodka. Maybe it wasn't the dark that was making me dizzy.

This is what we did for the five months we were partners. We showed up 3:30 to 5:00, Monday and Wednesday, for scheduled debate practice. We kept our heads in the game when the game was on. The rest of the time, including "special prep sessions" on Tuesday and Thursday, we laid on a pool table in the dark.

Sometimes we talked. Sometimes we fell asleep.

Sometimes we had sex.

When we did, it was just because.

The first time was a little awkward. *I* was a little awkward. It wasn't entirely pleasant. It certainly wasn't like the soft-core porn on afternoon soaps. When it was over, Corey said, "Now, you've got that off your conscience. Do you want to take a shower?"

A shower seemed like a great idea. I actually enjoyed it more than the sex.

There were no public displays of affection, because we both have our dignity. Let's call it dignity, what we had. It wasn't our dazzling social reputations; that's for sure.

. . .

On nights when his mom was home, we left the lights on, not that she ever came downstairs. Sometimes we watched TV, but that was harder than it should have been because we disagreed about what to watch. That was mostly my fault. I don't like much. I avoid feeding my brain anything that it can turn into nightmares—so the news, horror movies, and the weather channel are all out.

Corey was a little picky too. He was not amused by the CGI-enhanced-"documentaries" on the History Channel and made gagging noises when I got sucked into anything with subtitles. He said it proved I was a reading addict, especially when I would try to read the little white-print warnings and legal-weasel words that flashed across the screen during commercials. We shouldn't jump out of a plane to test the strength of magic glue? No shit, Sherlock, no shit.

We compromised on reality shows.

Corey enjoyed mocking the contestants. I was astonished at all the ways they could ruin their chances, whatever their chances were. Were they on drugs that scrubbed away their impulse control? Did they really think that peeing in someone else's shoes was a reasonable step in their plan for world domination of the dancing world? What made that woman think she could move a stack of several three-hundred-pound pumpkins filled with water and dry ice to the judging table? Could it really be legal to ask the contestants to swim around in a kiddie pool full of sewage sludge while looking for coins? Corey said I was naïve. Wasn't I paying attention when they said they weren't there to make friends? There was money and fame on the line. They were acting, mostly, playing a role.

Sometimes, I read while he killed virtual zombies. It gets to be white noise, after a little bit, the endless explosions. I just kept my eyes on the page in front of me so I didn't get CGI images of the creepy undead stamped on my retina.

Anyhow, we pissed away hours most nights.

. . .

Once, I went upstairs because Corey wanted an apple, but he didn't want to get it himself. He asked. I went.

When his mom said, "You must be Loa," she would have scared the pants off me, if I'd had any on. She was sitting all curled up and quiet as a cat on a big chair in a puddle of light. The rest of the house was dark.

"Yes," I said, and I pulled the T-shirt I was wearing down as far as I could over my butt.

"I'm glad Corey has a friend," she said. She didn't sound sarcastic. She didn't sound enthusiastic either. She took a sip out of a glass she held cradled in her fingers. The glass sparkled. "He's OK, isn't he? He's OK."

I just nodded, he seemed OK to me.

"I worry, you know?"

"He's OK," I said. "I'm just going to get him an apple."

"An apple?"

"He's OK. He just wants an apple."

She swirled her drink around in the glass and said, "Goodnight, honey." Then she switched off the lamp beside her and left us both in the dark.

I followed the light of the digital clock on the microwave into the kitchen, got Corey his damn apple, and took tiny, little baby steps to find my way downstairs in the night.

It was the only conversation I ever had with his mom. And during the times I was there, Corey never spoke to her at all.

. . .

"Rumor has it," Corey says, "that I'm gay."

I have nothing to say to that.

"Rumor has it," Corey says, "that you are planning to plant bombs in the girls' bathrooms and kill us all—at least those of us in the girls' bathrooms. And then you are going to sweep down the halls in a yellow slicker slaughtering innocents."

"A yellow slicker? The rodeo kind that makes the guys look like rubber ducks. Oooo! Fierce. Really fierce!"

"Well, you're crazy. That's the sort of thing that crazy people do."

"And what kinds of gay things are you doing?"

"Less than I'd like."

"So. You're gay."

"Gay as a tangerine. Gay as the Pillsbury Doughboy."

"Gay as a rodeo cowboy."

"Gay as Curious George."

"Was the Man in the Yellow Hat a pederast?"

"He was a monkey molester—and gay as lemon ricotta ravioli."

"I better start learning how to make pipe bombs."

"You'll be good at it."

"You know I will."

## Chapter 11

# Dark Matter

Antimatter is sort of like matter's evil twin,
Because, except for charge and handedness
  of spin,
They're the same for a particle and its anti-self.
But you can't store an antiparticle on any shelf,
Cuz when it meets its normal twin, they both
  annihilate.
Matter turns to energy, and then it dissipates.

—Alpinekat, "Large Hadron Rap"

Corey introduces me to the university library. It is vast and full of stuff. Some of it is interesting, and some of it is not. Theoretically, we are here to do research to make us better debaters, but to be honest, most of the stuff that ought to be helpful to us in debates falls into the "not that interesting" category.

I feel like I'm trespassing. Corey tells me I'm an idiot. It's a public place. It's a *library* for crap's sake. He asks if I feel guilty when I use toilet paper at the mall—do I feel like I'm stealing it? Do I leave pennies lined up on the back of the toilet to pay for every square? He doesn't know why he puts up with me, really he doesn't.

Then he winks and says we should go on the grand tour.

There is the Dewey decimal section. It is a ghetto for old books that couldn't just be put in the dumpster but weren't worth the trouble of assigning new numbers and moving to new shelves. There are the shelves of oversize books, exiled from their natural clans by their gigantism. Atlases, anatomy books, fashion portfolios, they are all tossed together and expected to get along. There are even books that defy being books. They are boxes of loose pages. There are others that have a single page folded inside.Unfolded, that page is a map as big as a bedsheet.

Corey showed me where they kept the little books of pornography—no, no, Corey said they were erotica, not porn—written by famous authors. They were much more interesting than a soap-opera romance or a TV ad selling cars or hamburgers or sex. Erotica, it turns out, is more about imagination than biological plumbing.

My favorites are the big glossy books of photography. I like the photo of a gray dog with a gray sock hanging from its nose. It's an elephant. On another page, the same dog is sitting quietly after someone poured a bag of flour or something all over it. There isn't a single trace of movement, not one paw print, in that flour. There is a woman who disguises herself again and again and makes portraits of each person she seems to be. There is a whole book of portraits of dead Wisconsinites: babies in long white gowns, criminals with bullet holes.

They are so different from the photographs I know. I know about *National Geographic* and family snapshots, that's all. Here I am with my second birthday cake. There I am with my dog, Ket, standing in a snowbank. My dad is in the picture too, but only as a pale blue shadow on the snow. You can tell he is the one taking the picture because of the way his shadow elbows are sticking out of his shadow head. Now I am holding a baby Asta wrapped up in her blanket. Where did I ever get a purple sombrero? And whatever happened to it?

And *National Geographic* is cool, but it's not the same as these books. I loved looking at the pictures of the woman who rode across Australia on a camel and the X-rays of Egyptian mummies, but this was different. The subject of these pictures was seeing. That's what they were about, seeing. They were not about dead babies or dogs dressed in golf sweaters. They were about looking and seeing.

I turn page after big glossy page. This is a whole new world. There are people who make a living just by showing other people what they see.

When Corey says it's time to go, I don't want to. He is pleased. I just want to keep looking at pictures, swallowing up other people's visions.

It is better than vodka.

. . .

I wanted to go the library again the next day, but Corey had different plans.

He said I needed a killer-bitch costume for debate. This worried me some, because the other girls in debate did not seem to be wearing black leather or spiked collars. Sometimes Corey's language was imprecise.

The next thing I knew, we were standing in his mother's closet and he was throwing clothes at me. There were no spiked collars involved, but that didn't make the experience better. Corey pulled a skirt off a hanger and flapped it at me.

"Maybe you could wear one on each leg?"

He pulled a sweater from the bottom of a neat, rainbow organized pile, "This could stretch," he said, while he stepped on one sleeve and pulled on the other, "Or not. You know, I think we are going to have to go to the mall."

I bent down to pick up the skirt he had tossed on the floor so I could hang it back up. Corey snatched it out of my hands and tossed it high onto a shelf. Then he flipped the whole pile of sweaters onto the floor.

"Leave it," he said.

And I did.

. . .

We went shopping.

The mall makes me miserable. I know it isn't supposed to, but it hurts my eyes and ears and gives me a headache. Too many reflections, too many places where music is coming at me from two directions at once. It just freaks me out.

Even though Corey seemed to know exactly what he was looking for, finding the debate costume of his dreams was difficult.

As for me, I lived through similar hell when I played Barbies with Reba in second grade. Endlessly shoving uncooperative arms into impossibly skinny sleeves: not fun. Chopping firewood builds biceps, and I chop a lot of firewood. Nothing fits right. My hair looked as frustrated as I felt. It floated around my head full of static electricity and all fratzed out from pulling things on and off.

Finally, though, Corey was satisfied. It was a charcoal gray suit. The skinny skirt wasn't short, but it fit tight. It had a slit up the back so I could walk a bit. The jacket, Corey announced, would create the illusion of an ass. And there were tall black boots with heels too.

When I came out of the fitting room I was surprised at Corey's face. When I looked in the three angled mirrors, I was even more surprised. I saw myself. Anyway I hoped it was myself. The only time I look in the mirror on purpose is when I brush my teeth. My self-image, as they say on *Oprah*, is a little warped. I'm used to seeing my hands doing what I tell my hands to do. I'm used to seeing my feet when I pull on my socks. But I am not used to seeing myself like this, a whole person.

The person in the mirror looked spooky good. Even with her wispy dark hair a mess, that person in the mirror looked like she could flick trouble out of her way like a bug. Her eyes looked level into mine. When I saw that person in the mirror, I stood different and I walked different. I felt different. And I liked it.

It may have been a coincidence, but my debate scores went up the first time I wore those clothes to a meet.

. . .

I liked not being home.

But I assumed that home was going to be there when I got back. One day, it wasn't.

It's not like the house burned down or an earthquake split the rock and swallowed everything whole. It was worse. More personal. My dog, Ket, died.

He was getting a little old. It took him a little longer to get up, especially on cold mornings. He never jumped off the porch to terrorize squirrels anymore. Still, he might have lived years and years, but he fell through the thin ice on the creek.

He probably just went down to get a drink, and when the ice broke, he wasn't quick enough to make it out. He didn't drown, but his back legs were swept under the ice by the water. He just hung on and struggled.

Little Harold found him there when he didn't come to get his dinner. Poor Little Harold. He tried, but he's just a little kid and he didn't have the strength. He just kept trying and crying until Dad went looking for him. Dad says we were just lucky that Little Harold didn't get trapped under the ice too.

All of this is secondhand knowledge. I didn't see it. I was having fun. I was at a speech and debate meet, racking up points. I was riding a bus through the snowy dark with a bunch of other speech and drama nerds. Ket never crossed my mind. Little Harold never crossed my mind. I never had a fleeting psychic moment where I looked at the icy world outside and shivered. I was perfectly, selfishly happy.

My dad was strong enough to fight the water and the ice, but he couldn't fight The Bony Guy.

. . .

Poor Little Harold slept all night on the floor by the woodstove with his arms around Ket's neck. When morning came, it was pretty clear that things weren't right. Ket didn't even try to get up.

By that afternoon, my dad had decided the only kind thing to do was put him down. Little Harold cried. Dad probably wanted to, but he just got the rifle and the dog into the truck and went to do what he had to do.

Sometimes I see shows on TV about paralyzed dogs that zip around in little wheeled carts or dogs that chase balls hopping along on their last two paws. Those stories don't make me smile. They always seem like a cruel joke. Ket's story ended so differently.

My dad stopped the truck on a logging road. Then he laid Ket out on the snow under a pine tree and shot him. That was the end of Ket. He was never going to gather us all up and keep us safe again.

Like I said, when I got home, home wasn't there anymore. Little Harold was sitting on his bed holding Ket's dish on his lap and crying. When I asked Dad where Ket was buried, he looked at me like I was stupid.

"The ground is frozen."

Sometimes when I ride my bike on the logging roads, I see bones. But they aren't Ket's bones. They are almost always from Bambi's stupid brothers. I may never find Ket. Bones don't last forever in the woods. Coyotes scatter them around. Mice and other little animals gnaw on them. They get chalky and start to break apart. Bones don't last forever.

But The Bony Guy does.

· · ·

The Bony Guy likes disguises.

*I am watching a late-night show. There is a guest who tried to pay for a cruise with a glossy photograph of the host. The host declares that it ought to be as good as money. It is a picture of him. People like him better than any of the guys on the money, don't they? The audience applauds wildly. Then he has a quiz for all of us. Question 1: Would you watch a bunny rabbit eat some lettuce? Question 2: Would you watch a bird peck something dead by the side of the road? Question 3: Would you watch dogs eat a live donkey? The audience applauds wildly.*

When I wake up. I am surprised I'm in bed. It certainly seemed like a real TV show.

. . .

"My mom is sending me to Europe."

Corey said it as if moms do that sort of thing, like they do laundry or nagging. Was it a summer vacation or something? I didn't know.

If you show me a map of Europe, I can name the countries. I can even name most of the capitals. In France the students riot and cars burn in the streets. In Spain the monument to the people killed by terrorists is peaceful. In England the endless stream in honor of the dead princess doesn't work very well and kids play in the water. Somewhere, protesters dye the water in a fountain red. What are they protesting? Animal fur in fashion, maybe? Or was it the genocide in Africa? I don't remember.

"I'm leaving next week," he said.

I said nothing. I had nothing to say.

"If I could take you with me I would, my pet," he said while he stroked my hair. "In a little pet carrier. I could get you a little pink collar with rhinestones on it. No—rhinestones and spikes—alternating. It would suit you better. During the day, I'll take you out for walks, and you can spend the nights whining in my room."

I knocked his hand away from my head so fast I pulled some of my own hair out. "Stop it. You don't have to be a jerk. I get it." I could hear him breathing in the dark.

"No, Pet, I don't think you do." Everything he says is so matter of fact—or so full of bullshit.

"Screw you!"

"That's right," he said. All I could hear was the tone. It's all, 'Who's a good doggie? Who is? Who?"

"Just leave me the fuck alone"

"That's what's happening, Loa. I'm leaving. I'm a jerk, and I'm leaving. And you're staying here. You're gonna hate me. Let's just get it started sooner." He was very matter of fact while he said this.

I just wanted to get away, but I'm clumsy, so I fell off the pool table and I couldn't find the light switch.

"Loa," he said, "Find your way out. We can see each other in the world someday."

I didn't stop to find out if he meant find my way out of his basement or find my way out of my crappy life and into the world where he was going.

I was glad his mother wasn't home so I didn't have to pass her, sitting in the dark, on my way out. I didn't have to seek her approval or disapproval or figure out what the hell was up with her. I just had to find my way out into the dark, and then I had to figure out what to do for the next few hours until it was time for school.

Twenty-four-hour restaurants are made for times like this.

I'm relatively clean. I had enough money to buy a cup of coffee, and I had something to read.

I didn't have enough money in my pocket to justify hours in a booth, but the waitress didn't know that. I'm not homeless or raving. She just filled my coffee cup and moved on. I had enough money to order some toast around 6:00 A.M. When I left, I put what change I had down for a tip. It wasn't much, but I had bought a place where it was warm and light and I could use the bathroom. I wanted her to know I appreciated her help. She might not have noticed though. Waitresses who work the graveyard shift must have their own problems.

· · ·

Corey wasn't in class the next day. Just like that, he was gone. And that was the end of the good old days. Again.

Debate was over for me. It was almost the end of the season anyway.

For a while, people who used to say "Hi" to Corey and me still said "Hi" to me without him, but I'd never really taken time to figure out who they were, and without Corey around, conversations just died.

A year before, Asta had died and left behind the emptiness where she had been. Now Corey had left behind another emptiness. It seems like emptiness shouldn't feel like anything, but I can tell you, when you touch the edges of emptiness, it aches.

# Chapter 12

## Constructive Interference

Imagine a lighthouse 10 m high has been constructed on Atlantis. Two tsunami waves are approaching from opposite directions and will arrive at the lighthouse at exactly the same time. One wave is 3.5 m high. The other is 5.5 m high. Will the flame at the top of the Atlantis lighthouse be extinguished?

My dad lost his job at the mill in April.

There have been rumors and talk for ages that the company was selling out. Things were going to change if that happened, everyone agreed on that. Nobody thought things would change for the better, and they didn't.

First, the mill was shut for twelve weeks so the new company could "evaluate their needs."

When that was over, they decided they didn't need my dad. He wasn't the only person they didn't need, but he wasn't really old, he wasn't a drunk, and he was a steady worker. My dad thinks he has it figured out why they didn't "need" him. He thinks it's because someone at some desk saw that there were a lot of medical bills for a child, Asta. Then they saw that there were more children on his policy. To the person at the desk, we must have looked like ticking time bombs waiting to explode in the mother-of-all insurance claims.

Fuckwits. If The Bony Guy didn't already install his magical destructive genes, we're safe.

We are welcome to continue our medical coverage, as stipulated by law. All we have to do is come up with $1,032 a month. Thank you so much for that. Can I just point out it might be a little hard, now my dad is out of work?

Fuckwits.

. . .

Mom got a job right away at Cozy Pines Residential Care. Lots of people must have applied during those first weeks after the mill closed, but most of those applicants had never given a sponge bath or a nasogastric feeding. Most of them probably didn't offer to take on-call work or say that the 11:00 P.M. to 7:00 A.M. shift was just fine.

Mom was such a good worker that they put me on weekends in the kitchen and dining room. It was not an enjoyable job, but I was lucky to have it, and that was quite clear every single time I got a paycheck.

Mom would sit at the kitchen table with the checkbook, a piece of scratch paper, and any bills that were waiting to be paid. It is one thing to be good at theoretical math; it's another thing, probably better, to be able to figure out how to skate from one week to the next without pissing anybody off or getting stuck in the Payday-Cash-Now-Check-Into-Cash hamster wheel of economic hell.

. . .

When summer came, I started scraping pre-chewed food into the garbage five days a week.

There were always four types of meals served at Cozy Pines: Regular, Soft, Whiz, and Liquid. The only meals that were ever finished completely were the Liquids, because those were poured directly into the resident, who had no more choice about it than a baby bird.

In the dining room, I served plates of Regular and Soft. I had to make sure there was never a saltshaker on the low-sodium table. Suicide by salt, can't have that. It would undo the dietitian's careful work. Each resident must have the healthful meal prescribed. A few could have coffee, a few more could have decaf. A few were never allowed grapefruit juice because it would interfere with their meds. Suicide by grapefruit juice, can't have that either.

I had to know who sat where and what they were permitted to eat. I had to know who was only permitted a blunt plastic butter knife—and I had to remind the cooks to cut things up on that plate.

I was not responsible for patients. It was up to others to get the residents to their places at the tables. It was up to others to make sure that there were no "events" during meals. In fact, while the actual eating was happening, I was allowed to return to the kitchen and eat my own meal. That was one of the fringe benefits of the job. We in the kitchen got meals for free.

Maybe it was because they thought we would steal food if it weren't allowed. Maybe it was a crude method of quality control. If so, it didn't work. The food was terrible, and the cooks, with keys to the walk-in freezer and the storeroom, were smart enough to stick to ice cream and peanut butter sandwiches. I ate the chopped meat patties (what animal? Who knows? "Meat" animal) and the overcooked veggies (soft enough for the Softs) and drank a quart of low-fat milk.

Then it was time to clear the plates, do the dishes, and mop the floor. Sounds snappy-fast when I say it like that, but I left out the details like stacking and carrying heaps of dishes in big rubber tubs. And washing the tables three times. And wiping up any spills before someone wandered in and slipped.

The next step was scraping the gobs off the plates and salvaging the occasional pair of dentures. It was much easier to capture those before they got moved to the dumpster. If I missed a pair of choppers, I would start my next shift in the dumpster picking through the bags of trash looking for the kitchen garbage and then feeling around blind until I found something hard in all that squishy crud.

I was a highly motivated worker.

Fill a rack, spray the dishes, slide them in the machine, fill a rack, spray the dishes, slide it through, but now it's twice as heavy because you have to push the clean dishes out.

Eventually, all the dishes are on the clean side and it's time to change aprons, take off the gloves, wash hands, and start returning stacks of plates and bowls to the shelves for the next meal. Silverware holds heat. My hands got used to it, the heat.

Then it was time to wash the pots and pans and serving items. Then it was time for the mop bucket and the three mops: one wet, one dry, one damp with disinfectant. Then I could shut the doors, turn off the lights, and leave. Unless I got done with my work too soon. I needed to put in a full four hours per shift. So if I hurried or if things weren't too messy, I had to spend any remaining time helping the cooks with prep for the next meal.

It was an experience worth avoiding. I did not have much in common with the cooks. I am not a widow, for example, and I've never found my husband pinned under the axel after the rig he was working on slipped off the blocks. I am not fascinated by whippets or *Judge Judy* or the guy in the blue and white trailer who is running a meth lab.

I just wanted to get out of the kitchen and get on my bike and enjoy a free ride down the hill to the highway. I could pick my own path: easy, hard, virtually impossible? Highway, skid road, deer path? Riding to work was never as much fun as riding home. I couldn't pooch around all night, but it was my free time.

· · ·

Dad picked up gyppo work as an independent sawyer when he could, but there were a lot of other guys trying to do the same. The woods are crawling with guys with chainsaws and shit-all chances of finding a job. Especially now with so many guys cut from the mill, and on top of that, they close the woods down for weeks in the summer to prevent fires.

Things would pick up when a fire broke out, because then Dad could get on a fire crew and bring in some money. It is weird to think about a forest fire as good luck, but that's the way it is. A fire means they need guys on the fire lines. A forest fire means a shot at a job for a while. A forest fire is way better than a scratch-off lottery ticket.

So far, only Texas and California were burning up— grass fires and urban fires—not my dad's area of expertise. So he and Little Harold were roaming up and down the creeks fishing. Judging by the remains in the frying pans, the two of them were living on trout. It's good food for cheap, if you have the time, and they had nothing but time.

. . .

We had our new orbits. Things were reasonably settled.

Then I screwed it up.

. . .

I'm a little late for work, so I just blast down a hill from a gravel road onto the paved highway. In front of a car. Really. Or maybe I hit the car. I don't know. I will be the first person to admit that all I was watching was the patch of dirt directly in front of my bike tire, and I wasn't even thinking about that. The next thing I know, I'm in the barrow pit on the opposite side of the pavement. My bike is halfway back up the hill. One wheel is still spinning, and the other one is bent like a fortune cookie.

Some guy is leaning over me saying, "Loa! Loa! Are you OK?"

And I'm thinking, "Who the hell is this guy?" and "How does he know my name?" He's a nice guy, though. And he seems genuinely worried. He's so worried that I start to worry myself: Do I have bones sticking out of me? Are my brains leaking out of my ears? I manage to get up on my hands and knees and then wobble up onto my feet. I can't see any bones sticking out.

"Are you OK?" The guy is still asking. He still looks worried. He looks familiar.

I realize he was in my sophomore English class last quarter of last year. We even made a video together. It was a stop-motion movie about mannequins in a park. Mannequins feeding squirrels, mannequins throwing away trash, mannequins mugging and murdering people. Don't ask me what it was about. I wasn't the director. Neither was the nice guy who is hovering over me all worried. I can't remember his name. I remember I thought he was stupid as a rock balloon at first. Then I thought he was kind of funny.

"I'm OK," I straighten up and look at my bike. "I've got to go to work."

"You should go to the hospital. You might be really hurt. I'll give you a ride," says the nice guy from film class.

"No. I work right up there." I point to Cozy Pines Residential Care where it sits overlooking the river

"I'll take you there then," says nice guy. And I let him because I don't want to drag my mangled bike down the barrow pit and up the driveway to Cozy Pines.

But when I actually walk in the service entrance to the kitchen, I'm not feeling so good. The adrenaline has drained out of my muscles and left me sore and shaking. The cooks look at me funny. So I look at myself. My kitchen uniform is all dirty, ripped, and bloody on the shoulder and all down one leg. The head cook says to see the nurse at the desk, and the nurse at the desk says I do have to go to the emergency room to be checked out. It's OK, she says, because I've got worker's insurance, but I will lose my wages for the day's work. One of the aides will drive me, and they will call my mom and tell her what's going on.

I just go because missing work seems OK at the moment. I'm sick of work.

At the emergency room, they check me out and say nothing is broken. I don't have a concussion. I'm no emergency. I'm no big deal. I'm just some scrapes and bruises and muscle strain. A nurse wearing scrubs with palm trees and smiling suns in sunglasses bandages me up and gives me a prescription for painkillers. When she hands me the prescription, she gives me the stern stink eye for a moment and then says, "This is for you, not anybody else."

Like people get in bike wrecks for pain meds. Come to think of it, maybe they do, but it doesn't seem worth it to me.

Then I'm well enough to wait in the lobby until my mom comes to collect me. The TV is on twenty-four-hour news. The world is burning down, melting, and flooding. Pretty much like yesterday and the day before that.

When my mom comes in, she is all pale and rattled—until she sees me—then she is just mad.

"How the hell are we going to pay for this?"

I don't know. I don't say that. I don't want to say anything. Does everyone in the world think I get in bike wrecks on purpose?

"The charge nurse said I have insurance."

"The charge nurse *has* insurance. She is full-time professional. You are not. Shit! *I* don't even have insurance from Cozy Pines."

Mom goes to the desk to talk about payment. Little Harold comes close and gives me a hug. I don't know what hurts worse, my shoulder or that Little Harold wants to take care of me. Who am I kidding? Ripping some skin off is nothing compared to the idea that he wants to take care of me. I should be taking care of him, and we both know it.

. . .

"Did they give you a prescription?" Mom asks. Her hands are tight on the steering wheel. Her knuckles are white, but the rest of her hands are chapped and red. It's an occupational hazard of nursing home work. Endless hand washing, gloving up to change diapers, placing bedpans, harsh disinfectants, cold weather, hot water. Whenever I see red hands, I remember Asta. I don't want to remember Asta.

I pull the prescription out of my pocket and hand it to Mom.

"You don't need this," she says, "Just take some aspirin. This crap will make you sleepy and constipated." Then she puts the prescription in her coat pocket.

I choose to believe that my mom is not one of the people at Cozy Pines who takes the old people's meds for fun or profit. I know they exist. They peel the pain patches right off those old achy bodies. Sometimes they cut up the patches and scrape out the inside. Sometimes they just pop the whole patches in their mouths and chew on them like gum. It's easier to come by than Oxycontin, and not everyone enjoys meth.

God knows, my mom probably hurts. She could probably use a little release. But I choose to believe that she would never leave someone else hurting by stealing meds—not even me.

## Chapter 13

# Features of the Summer Sky

The two largest planets in the solar system will share the sky this month. Ringed Saturn will appear in the west and will set shortly after the sun. Saturn may seem a little less impressive than you may have seen it in the past. This is because the rings are tilted so they reflect less light from the sun. Jupiter, however, will be a noticeable bright "star" when it rises in the eastern sky.

After my accident, the new deal was this: Mom drove me to work, but I had to walk home.

The new deal was also this: my shoulder hurt like hell.

It was really hard to carry the tubs of dishes and push the racks through the machines. That was my problem.

My visit to the emergency room cost two weeks' wages. That was the whole family's problem.

Walking home sucked.

My problem.

When a truck pulled over on the shoulder in front of me and the door swung open, that seemed like a great deal.

I was hot and sweaty and I smelled like Cozy Pines, which isn't good. The truck door was open, and there was Esther, smiling. Her brother, Abel, was in the driver's seat. Abel never smiled, but he had pulled the truck over, so I climbed in. It wasn't cool in the truck, but the air moving through the open windows felt good.

Where were we going? I didn't care anymore than the dogs running from side to side in the bed of the truck. I was so happy not to be walking down the ditch by the highway, I wouldn't have refused to go to their weird-ass church with them at that moment if it meant I could get a ride home afterwards. As it turned out, though, church wasn't where we were going.

. . .

There were seven or eight rigs at the campground. It amounted to a pretty good-sized crowd. Most of them were people who had gone to the same grade school. I recognized people who had used me like a sled dog when I was little. Seriously, the big kids used to tie us to sleds with baling twine and make us mush, dragging them along. I'm not a puppy anymore, I guess. I'm running with the big dogs now.

I don't know who arranged for the beer, but there it was, an aluminum keg on a stump. The sun was starting to drop behind the mountains, but it wouldn't be full dark for hours yet. The creek running through the clearing was bone-shocking cold, but it felt good when I splashed my face and arms.

Out of nowhere, things had suddenly improved.

After the second cup of beer, my shoulder didn't hurt so much anymore.

I sat on the tailgate of Abel's truck with Esther. She was drinking too but a lot more slowly. We didn't talk. Esther always had kind of a gift of silence. She never said much, and she never made me feel like I had to say anything either. It's sort of uncommon, the ability to be quiet.

By the time the moon came up, I had a pretty good buzz. Some of the kids decided to go into town, so I caught a ride down the road and had them drop me off near home.

Nobody was there when I got to the house.

Mom was at work.

I had no idea where Dad and Little Harold were.

It didn't really matter.

I took a shower and some aspirin and went to sleep.

I didn't dream at all.

I was the luckiest girl in the world.

· · ·

"How did you spend your summer vacation?"

I spent the morning doing housework at home and afternoons working like a machine at Cozy Pines. Then I spent the nights out in a bunch of different hidden places along the logging roads drinking beer and being as normal as I could figure out how to be.

Mostly, I got there with Abel and Esther.

I never really understood how beer and bonfires fit in with the rules they had to follow. The closest I ever came to asking was one night when Esther and I were sitting on the hood of the truck watching the stars come out.

"Star light, star bright," I said.

"And God said, 'Let there be lights in the expanse of the sky to separate the day from the night, and let them serve as signs to mark seasons and days and years, and let them be lights in the expanse of the sky to give light on the earth.' And it was so. God made two great lights—the greater light to govern the day and the lesser light to govern the night. He also made the stars," said Esther.

I pointed to the brightest light in the sky and said, "That's Jupiter. It's a planet."

"In the Bible, it's a star," said Esther, and she smiled and took another sip of beer.

She looked happy. She was happy. There was no good reason for me to make her unhappy, and insisting that the

Bible had it wrong or asking questions about her home life and her parents would probably have done just that. So I let it go.

I doubt that Abel and Esther provided all the details to their dad, but I didn't go out of my way to tell my mom and dad exactly how I was spending my time either.

It wasn't like we were the first kids to get drunk in those places. Our parents probably had keggers there twenty years ago. This isn't a deep mystery or new development. They probably figured we were safer at a campground or some logging road than we would have been on the highways.

There were some driving miscalculations, to be sure. I thought it was kind of fun when someone got high-centered or backed up too far and dropped a wheel off the edge of the road. There were always enough of us that we could work it out. It feels pretty cool, actually, to be working with people and to be able to move a rig back up on the road.

Of course, we were out on the highways too.

. . .

That, actually, was the one thing my parents would have been hard-assed about, drinking and driving on the highway. It isn't an irrational concern, and honestly, I avoided it.

I have no death wish. I do not think I am bulletproof. Since the bike wreck, it is pretty clear to me that mistakes happen. So I was cautious. But I was also happy to have a life of my own. I liked seeing people. I liked drinking beer and being out in the woods. And I really liked having something to look forward to when I was washing dishes at Cozy Pines because, without that, the job would have been even worse.

Then, in late August, the sun turned red behind a skin of smoke. There were fires in Idaho. It was the break we had been waiting for all summer, and Dad needed to go.

"Good-bye, Dad, make lots of money and don't get caught at the wrong time in the wrong place."

I never really said that. It's too real, the chance that a guy, a crew, will get caught when a fire blows up when the wind shifts.

All the guys on the fire lines carry shelters now. That's what they call those flimsy little tube tents of shiny foil—shelters. When the fire is coming, it's time to scrape a bare spot in the mineral soil and climb in. The shiny surface is supposed to reflect the heat. As long as you don't move, as long as you stick your nose in the dirt and don't try to run when the fire starts to roar overhead and blister your skin, and as long as the fire doesn't steal the air right out of your lungs, the fire shelter is supposed to keep you safe. The guys make jokes about baked potatoes. I say nothing about baked potatoes when I say good-bye to Dad.

A fire could take off right here at home, of course. If it does, we get the hell out fast. That is all. No heroic stand with a gravity-feed garden hose from the creek. I don't have it in me. I saw a deer once that had been caught in a fire. It was rigid and black and something pink—brains?

blood?—had boiled out of its nose after the burning was done. I have no interest in dying like that.

I have no interest in dying at all.

· · ·

I don't think Little Harold had been in the shower for a month. He smelled like a hot puppy rolled in angleworms and trout slime. He was very brown, even after I got the dirt washed off. Dad didn't take the whole sunscreen thing very seriously.

It was fun to be with him again, to tickle his skinny ribs and watch cartoons on TV with him. The last few days of summer slid by like that: work, home, the smell of burning forests, and a red cherry sun floating through the sky.

Chapter 14

# RIP: Dolly the Sheep, 1996–2003

Dolly the sheep had a short career. Most sheep have a life span of twelve years, but by the age of six, Dolly suffered the physical deterioration of a sheep twice her age. Of course, Dolly was no ordinary sheep. She was a clone. Some scientists think that her early demise was directly linked to her unusual origin—since she had been created from a cell taken from a six-year-old sheep, Dolly the lamb was born old. Cloning may be the only way to create a new woolly mammoth, but when it comes to creating sheep, old-fashioned sexual reproduction is the cheapest, easiest, and most dependable route.

Sometimes I learn something new before I even get to homeroom. There are these glass display cases that clubs and teachers use to advertise their particular obsessions. For example, there is the giant bottle full of fruit flies. First, there were only two and now—Oh! The flymanity!—crowds living off corpses. It's a zombie-apocalypse movie but with fruit flies.

Today I notice a new display.

"??? Are you REALLY ready for SEX ???"

It's an interesting question. I don't have a condom in my pocket. I no longer have a friend-with-privileges.

"??? Am I ready for SEX ???"

Um, No. That's the answer they want, but not the reasons.

The case is filled with old kitchen and housekeeping stuff. A metal dishpan filled with china teacups and a cast iron frying pan, the kind of iron you had to sit on a woodstove to heat, a washboard. . . . A washboard? What is the message here? Does sex lead to time travel or what? Have sex, spend the rest of your life so deep in the past you have to wash underpants by hand. There is a big cockeyed baby doll propped in the corner. Do you really want to spend the rest of your life changing diapers? And washing them with a washboard? Only if you're married. That's the point. Somehow, being married will make the cock-eyed baby and the laundry and the cooking and the dishes and the diapers so much fun.

This is the sort of time when Corey used to say, "Take a moment to pity the stupid." I hear his voice in my head. I miss him.

. . .

By the third week of this school year, the routine was clear. I rode the bus to school. I got off the bus and went to my classes. I got back on the bus and went home.

I still had my job at Cozy Pines. No more weekday shifts though; I couldn't get there on time. It was just going to be weekends and holidays for lucky me.

Then Friday came around, and I was sitting on a tailgate watching the river current. The water looked thick and ropy as melted glass. I could feel the cold seeping through my jeans. I had a little slice of time I thought belonged to me, just to me, between school and work on Saturday.

I heard the tires squeal.

I heard a blunt thud.

Sometimes I wonder if I really heard that sound, the sound of the truck hitting Esther. Could I really have heard that sound, separated from the rest of the crash? Or did my memory just make that up, to help me try to understand the sequence of events? Do I just remember a blunt thud because I think there ought to have been one?

. . .

There are infinite universes, and each has its observers. A Freak Observer pops into existence as a self-aware entity that makes its universe orderly. Do you ever wonder why time doesn't run backwards? Do you ever wonder why gravity is always on? Freak Observer. Freak Observer. Freak Observer. We owe it all to the Freak Observer. At least I think we do.

This is my universe, and I am bound to observe it.

I have watched babies—both my Asta and Little Harold—discover the world. For weeks they just look and look. Sometimes they cry. They eat and they get their diapers changed. Then they find their hands. It's an amazing thing. They go cross-eyed from concentration. They stare so intently at their hands. One hand touches the other. They get the hand into their mouth, and they are so intense. Honestly, I have seen teenage boys having sex, and they aren't even so intense as babies who are figuring out that they have hands . . . and mouths . . . and the world.

So I have seen how observers are born into the world.

And I have seen how an observer dies.

**Chapter 15**

# C
## E N
### S O R
### S H I P
### C A U S E S
#### B L I N D N E S S

Can YOU see WHO is Blinding YOU?
READ!

I have to find a poem for English class. The whole class does. We have all been turned loose in the library on a scavenger hunt, an Easter egg hunt, and we are supposed to bring poems back. Song lyrics don't count. There was much griping about that little point.

I don't know why Ms. (Heartless) Hart hates the librarian, but apparently she does. She shepherded us all through the halls and into the library. Then she disappeared.

Today there are people in the library who are never in the library. They just want to get this over with quickly. They swarm the help desk. I'd say "like maggots," but they are noisy and calling out for poems about beer and suicide and vampires and baby deer. Maggots are pretty quiet, in my experience. I am quiet like a maggot. I don't even ask for help. I pretend that I'm working on poetry, but instead, I'm writing about noisy maggots.

. . .

I haven't spoken to my dad for a long time. We have nothing much to say. He tells me no stories. I ask him no questions. We don't smile.

Tonight, though, I said, "I need a poem. A poem about stars."

He got up from the kitchen table and went to the shelves in the living room. He doesn't search around. He goes right to the place on the shelf and pulls out a little book. He opens it and hands it to me:

*Stars at Tallapoosa*

*The lines are straight and swift between the stars.*
*The night is not the cradle that they cry,*
*The criers, undulating the deep-oceaned phrase.*
*The lines are much too dark and much too sharp.*

*The mind herein attains simplicity,*
*There is no moon, no single, silvered leaf.*
*The body is no body to be seen*
*But is an eye that studies its black lid.*

*Let these be your delight, secretive hunter,*
*Wading the sea-lines, moist and ever mingling,*
*Mounting the earth-lines, long and lax, lethargic.*
*These lines are swift and fall without diverging.*

*The melon-flower nor dew nor web of either*
*Is like to these. But in yourself is like:*
*A sheaf of brilliant arrows flying straight,*
*Flying and falling straightaway for their pleasure,*

*Their pleasure that is all bright-edged and cold;*
*Or, if not arrows, then the nimblest motions,*
*Making recoveries of young nakedness*
*And the lost vehemence the midnights hold.*

　　—*Wallace Stevens*, Harmonium, *1922*

My dad doesn't say anything. He doesn't help me read. He doesn't explain anything.

He doesn't have to, I guess. I have never seen the ocean, so I'm not really sure about sea-lines, but I have seen the stars. And they aren't really like dew or webs or what I guess a melon-flower might be. They are stars. I know that starlight travels in a straight line for longer than my whole life to reach my eye—but my eye being here is purely accidental. If I blink, that light is gone forever.

That has to be good enough.

. . .

So I read the poem in Ms. (Heartless) Hart's class. She calls on me near the end of the period. If I had a longer poem, it would have been cut in half by the bell. As it is, she asks me a question, "What does that mean, Loa?" She never asked anyone else that question. Everyone else got a round of applause for being able to stand up and make the sound of words. I did that. It isn't good enough.

So I answer, "The stars shine, and it doesn't matter if we see them or not."

The bell rings.

Ms. (Heartless) Hart raises her voice, "Loa. Where did you get that poem?"

"From home," I say. I hand her the photocopy with the bibliographic citation—as required by the assignment.

"I can't give you the library research credit."

I say nothing. She bent the rules for the mouthbreathers who brought song lyrics, but she can't bend the rule for having a dad who reads poetry. Understood.

For just a moment, she's looking me in the eye. I pretend I can see right through her retina into the flabby jelly behind it. I don't flinch.

. . .

When the snow comes, it's the light and not the cold that lets you know.

My dad says that snow is how you know if you are a kid. If it makes you happy, you're a kid. It's that simple.

But maybe it's not. I remember the first time snow made me cry, and I was very little—only in the first grade.

It came in the night, while I was sleeping. I'm pretty sure my mom and dad both knew. They needed to keep the house warm. They kept an eye on the weather. They might have known it was coming because Ed the smiling weatherman told them it was coming—or they might have seen how the clouds were acting. But I was little. It wasn't my job then to keep the fire going. The only weather reports that matter were the ones my mom dished out with breakfast, "Eat your oatmeal. It's going to be cold today," or "You are going to be hot as a monkey in that stupid sweatshirt."

I woke up, and the world was white. So what? It happens. Snow happens. But when I went downstairs, Mom said there wasn't going to be any school. Silly Mom. It was only Wednesday. Wednesday is library day. Wednesday is a school day for sure.

Mom said, "No school."

I cried.

It was Wednesday. Library day. I needed to swap my books in. Wednesday is library day. She was wrong. I was right. I found my own boots. I zipped my own coat. I was right. It was library day.

I opened the kitchen door and stepped out onto the porch. I couldn't go any farther. The snowbanks were in my way.

Mom grabbed my arm and dragged me into the kitchen.

"Harold," said Mom, "You deal with this." She pointed at me.

Dad came to the doorway. He looked at me. He looked at me a long time.

"OK," he said. "You wait here."

I waited in the kitchen. I was still crying, but I was being quieter about it.

"C'mere," Dad yelled.

I went out the door. He had his snowshoes. He picked me up and put me on his shoulders. I remember that he did that, but I don't remember how it felt. I wasn't crying anymore. I was happy. I was going to school.

We went across the creek and through the woods. It's shorter to the highway that way than it is if you follow the road.

But when we got to the highway, it wasn't there. All there was was snow. I know it was the bus stop, but there wasn't any highway. There weren't any cars. Dad just stood there with me on his shoulders. It was so quiet. I could hear trees breaking under the snow. I knew then that the bus wasn't going to come. So I cried.

I cried all the way home.

When we got there, Dad put me down and told me to go in the house.

Mom wiped my nose and took off my coat.

I just stood there in my boots and snow pants. I sucked each breath in a long sniff and let it out in a wail.

My mom wiped my nose again and put her warm hands against my face and tipped my head so we were looking at each other eye to eye.

"Don't be an idiot," she said. "If you don't stop crying, you are going to make yourself sick. And you're making the dog sad."

Dad came in. I turned my bawling self toward him. After all his effort so far, I still expected him to fix it. I still thought there must be some way to go to school.

Dad walked right past me and opened the closet under the stairs. After a little rummaging and swearing, he pulled out a cardboard box full of yellow books. Then he pulled out another. He put them close to the heating stove.

"Read these," he said.

So I did. I read *National Geographic* for five days straight. I didn't know what the hell I was reading about most of the time. I mostly just looked at the pictures. I learned though. I learned a girl can ride camels across the desert in Australia. I learned that tulips have tiny seeds, and Newton was a silver-haired man interested in rainbows. And I learned that there are stars in the sky that I can't see.

. . .

I've been going to the library during lunch and whenever else I can make an excuse to be there. I look for information on two problems. Problem 1 is the Freak Observer. What is it really? Is it a real thing or just a fairy tale of physics? At this point, I don't have any confidence in my understanding. Problem 2 is getting rid of The Bony Guy. Honestly, there is squat-all on the library shelves that is useful to me, but the Internet helps.

Today the focus is Problem 2, subpart A: dreams.

It's hard to find useful stuff about dreams. I have to dig through a lot of crap about what things "symbolize."

Like dream dictionaries. A dream dictionary is a one-size-fits-all-palm-reading-astrology-column-in-the-newspaper-carrot-equals-penis secret-code decoder. On the plus side, the next time I need to write an essay for Ms. (Heartless) Hart, I could probably just plagiarize from a dream dictionary like this, "I think the Nazis in the book represent an evil and merciless force that cannot be reasoned with. They represent the sorts of people who put other people down." It might be an interesting experiment. I can see a couple of possible outcomes. Maybe Ms. (Heartless) Hart would be happy with an essay like that. It would prove that she was getting through to me.

Or maybe she would break out the red ink to circle those prepositions at the ends of the sentences. But that is about the only use I can imagine for the handy-dandy dream dictionaries. They are useless as tits on a tomcat when it comes to getting rid of The Bony Guy.

I'm not interested in doing literary criticism of my dreams. I am the poet here, and I know what it means when I find Asta's slipper in the snow. The snow in my dreams isn't about "isolation" or "innocence." It was February when my sister died. I live in a world where it snows.

. . .

I find it weird that nobody teaches us about dreams in school. You'd think it would come up at some point, like maybe in health class or something, but it doesn't. There was that inspirational speaker who tore a phone book in half and told us to dream big, but his message had nothing to do with our dream life while we sleep. He was all about goals and, I guess, dislike for phone books.

It's like everyone is living this other life, full of creepy shit, and the whole thing is totally ignored.

As far as that goes, thinking, in general, is pretty much ignored. Nobody ever said to me, "We are going to learn about thinking, now. We are going to learn how to learn."

I mean, they told me stuff like "Chicken, airplane, soldier" to help me learn to swim. There were little movies about how to wash my hands and brush my teeth. They provided step-by-step directions on—duh, duh,

DUH!—using tampons, but as for the care and feeding of my brain, nothing.

I'm on my own.

. . .

It's pretty new science, the science of dreams, and there isn't much consensus.

Still, there are some facts: At least 25 percent of trauma victims have repetitive dreams of the event with feelings of intense rage, fear, or grief. About the same number of children have nightmares with frightening, detailed plots.

Adults don't have nightmares as much, unless they have "thin-boundary creative personalities"—or they are batshit crazy. It's nice to have options.

I'm not sure where I fit in all of this. I don't know where to put my data point on the chart. Am I a normalish child turning into a screwed-up adult? Am I "creative"? Or crazy? Maybe when I can read these research papers without feeling like a dog in high heels. . . . It appears to be English. I mean, *frequency*, *magnitude*, and *correlation* are all English words. *Lucid* usually means "clear and easy to understand," but not when it comes to dreams. Here it means that the person dreaming is aware that they are dreaming. I think. People can even make stuff happen in their dreams. I think. So I guess the point is, I should just keep having nightmares because there is a chance I might be able to be a lucid dreamer someday. Lucky me.

## Chapter 16

# CARTOON PHYSICS

Gravity never applies until the cat/dog/coyote looks down.

Reba slides into the bus seat beside me. This is the first time she has sat beside me on purpose since we were in sixth grade.

Reba never had any identity crisis. Her mom's been dressing her like a wanna-be buckle bunny since she was eight, and Reba is OK with that. Reba loves her momma. They dance to the same music, share clothes, and they're both trying to stop smoking by using the patch.

I know this because Reba talks a little loud on the bus. She can afford to. Everybody on Bus 32 loves Reba, especially J.B. the bus driver. What's not to love about a girl who pushes her jeans down to show you a nicotine patch? Especially when she announces that she put it on her ass so nobody would see it. And I love Reba too, because I remember when we were in the Mother's Day Tea program when we were six and we dressed up like mice. She helped me pull out my first wiggly tooth. What's not to love about the girl who was brave enough to reach in and jerk a baby tooth right out of my mouth? And whatever anybody says about Reba, she has all her shit kicked into a pile. I can't say the same about myself.

"You know that gay guy you were hanging with?" Reba asks.

"You mean Corey?"

"Whatever, that guy, you know." She pulls her phone out of her jeans pocket and flips it open. She lowers her voice and leans a little closer so I can see the screen.

There on that two-inch screen is Corey. Not just Corey.

"This guy I kinda know found this on the net. That guy, Corey, had tagged it with our high school and a bunch of other shit. It was like he *wanted* the whole school to see it.

I'm just staring at the little tiny screen. I would like to be disinterested, but I really need to see this. We are on the pool table in his basement. Those night vision cameras work, but Corey's eyes shine like the eyes of a lion eating a gazelle by a dark waterhole. The camera angle doesn't show my face.

"Who does he think he is? Paris Hilton? Or is she supposed to be Paris Hilton? That's not Paris Hilton. That girl's thighs are *ginormous*."

"Is there more?"

"Not that I know. But this is just skeezy. That guy is skeezy. He might not be gay, but he is skeezy as hell. I'm glad you're not still seeing him."

"Thanks. You don't have to worry. He's gone. Completely gone."

In a moment, Reba will hop from my seat to a better one. J.B. the bus driver never yells at her not to change seats while the bus is moving, but he takes his eyes off the road and stares in the interior mirror to watch her ass while she moves to the back of the bus.

When we get to my bus stop, I get off, and I and my ginormous thighs start the hike up the hill toward home.

. . .

I'm waiting for the other boot to drop. You know, waiting
for weird looks and whispers or for a copy of the image
Corey posted to get taped to my locker—some such shit.
It still hasn't happened. Nothing's happened. Yet.

What's Corey's deal?

When I get some time on the library computer, I
Google myself. Next to nothing. A couple of mentions for
last year's state AA speech and debate, that's it. There are
5,610 results for chiffon wombat. There are 21,200 hits for
hydraulic bandana. There are 14,500 hits for ginormous
thighs, but none of them are mine.

. . .

The chickens are all dead. The predator in some of the
cases is open to debate. It might have been a weasel or a
mink that got into the pen and killed the first three. Mom
got the rest.

The smell of burning feathers sits in the air.

Mom is near the woodshed with a pile of dead birds by
her feet. When I was little, she explained that they don't
feel it so much if you just whack the head off fast, with
a sharp ax. I guess she still believes that, judging by the
bloody heads scattered in the chips by the chopping block.
She has a tub of water boiling, waiting for the next chicken
to scald. She throws handfuls of feathers into the garbage
barrel. The feathers don't blow around or do any of the
other things feathers usually do, they are just wadded-up,
soggy gobs that stick to my mom's hands.

Feathers get wet when you butcher chickens.

You hold the headless chicken by its feet and lower it into soapy boiling water for a quick dip. This loosens the feathers, but you have to be careful to make it quick. If you go slow, the bird will start cooking. That would be just nasty. When you pull the bird out, you have to start pulling the feathers off. Wet feathers stink. But burnt feathers stink worse. You have to use fire to singe the last little feathers off. It is handy to roll up some newspaper and use that since you don't want a real hot fire. Again, you don't want to cook the bird. That would be just nasty.

Once all the feathers are off, then it's time to open the bird up and get rid of the guts. Mom likes to eat the hearts and livers, so she sorts those out and sets them aside like slimy little treasures. I guess the hearts are OK but chewy. I have nothing good to say about the livers.

"Some god-damned thing got in the chicken house," says Mom. "I'll be damned if whatever the fuck it is is going to get any more of *my* god-damned chickens."

It occurs to me that my mom is pretty drunk. She is having a bad day.

"I'll go change clothes, and then I'll help you."

"You can start by cleaning the dead ones out of the pen."

"Will do."

. . .

Little Harold is sitting in front of the TV eating a bowl of cereal. On TV a cartoon cat just noticed it has run over the edge of a cliff. Gravity never applies in cartoons until the cat looks down.

"I am never eating anything but cereal again. And milk," says Little Harold. "Cows don't mind about the milk, do they?"

"Don't worry," I say, "It doesn't hurt the cows." I love him too much to mention how most cows live these days.

How could a boy who spent his summer poking around in the entrails of little trout to see what they had been eating get so squeamish all of a sudden? I think it has something to do with seeing Mom out there, flecked with blood and with wet feathers stuck to her arms. That'd do it, seeing Mom looking all crazy and murdering her own chickens.

"I have to go out and help now."

"I'll save you some cereal."

"Thanks."

. . .

I reach into the mailbox and pull out the junk mail and bills. It's my job to pick up the mail. The bus drops me right by the row of mailboxes, so I take it home with me. Junk mail and bills—and a postcard addressed to me.

It is weird how much that girl on the postcard looks like me. Nobody ever says I look like anybody. I do not resemble any TV stars or cover girls or the weather girl on the local station. I don't even resemble my Depression-era ancestors staring out of the pictures on the walls at home. But this painting, that face, it looks like me. I have those full cheeks, that round chin. I have a frown around my eyes most of the time. I'm not the smiling type.

The girl with a face like mine is wearing a white turban and a shiny white dress tied together with strings and ribbons, but not too tied together. It looks like her boobs are going to fall out if she takes a deep breath. The girl with a face like mine is mad as hell. She has a hammer and a big nail in her hand. A poor old refugee from Cozy Pines is sitting behind her, praying and staring at heaven. She reminds me of Anna, who sits by the big window all day catching flies and eating them. At the very back of the painting, there is the face of a dark man. He looks mildly amused.

On the back, it says that this is Jaël of the Old Testament, painted by Salomon de Bray in 1635.

Fancy meeting you here...
Love,
Corey

Nothing about little pictures of sex on the pool table. Nothing.

. . .

When I do a search on Jaël on the library computer, I learn she drove a tent peg through a guy's head as an act of hospitality. The drift of the story is that he deserved it. It isn't clear how Jaël would have known that. Maybe she didn't. Maybe she just got lucky, and the one time she decided to nail some guy's skull to the dirt, God approved.

. . .

I wish I were Jaël—or even looking at her picture in a museum far away, but I'm not. I'm here. I'm in a school bus full of noise and the smell of dirty wool hats. When I walk through the hall, I avoid Mrs. Bishop's eye because my grades are slipping and I'm pretty sure neither of us wants to talk about it. All I have in my future is pulling another murdered chicken out of the freezer and turning it into soup that Little Harold won't eat.

## Chapter 17

# Practice in Visualization

Sketch a plan for a physics-related Halloween costume. Although it will not be judged on artistic merits, it should be a clear visualization of a concept or theory. Make certain to include units of measurement where appropriate. (The Doppler effect is not a costume choice for the purpose of this assignment. Show a little creativity here, people.)

Last year Little Harold begged and begged to go into town to go for trick or treating. Trick or treating around here sucks for a little kid. It is way too cold and dark to walk to anybody's house, and once you got there, they probably wouldn't know it was Halloween.

"Trick or treat! Isn't that nice, here's a dime."

"Want a beer, kid?"

"Get the fuck off my porch or I'll sic the dogs on you, you little shit!"

When I was twelve, I went into town with Reba and her mamma one Halloween and I got a whole pillowcase full of candy. It's no wonder that Little Harold thinks trick or treating in town is the Holy Grail. Or at least, he thought so last year. This year he hasn't mentioned it.

Yesterday, I asked him what he wanted to do. I made it clear we probably couldn't do it, but I was just interested.

"I think I outgrew that," he said.

He outgrew Halloween? I didn't know what to say. It made me feel terrible hearing that, but it's not like I can tell him he should get his hopes up. It's not like I can say, "Hey! Halloween is going to be great this year." It's going to suck. He knows it. He's over it.

He dumped some cold cereal in a bowl. There wasn't quite enough milk. He spilled what there was on top of the cereal, and then he put in a little water and stirred it around. I guess he's got things figured out. It makes me sad to think that. I realize I have been using him as a source of optimism. I'm like some greedy vampire who just noticed I sucked a corpse dry. There isn't any little-kid happiness left in Little Harold. I can't live off his cheerfulness anymore.

. . .

Today I exercise my privilege to leave the school grounds at lunch. We have "open campus"—doesn't that sound more dignified than "open prison"? Oooo, fancy! But I never left school during the day before. Not even when I was hanging out with Corey. He thought it was weird that I wouldn't even leave the school to find human food alternatives to the cafeteria chow. I thought it was weird to want to leave. I would have gone crazy worrying about being late for my next class.

I guess I'm a little braver now, or stupider. I cross the street to the Quickee-Mart and choose a big sack of fun-size candy bars.

"Binge and purge, huh?" The guy at the counter thinks he's funny. He doesn't deserve an answer.

After I get home, I wait until Little Harold is deeply plugged into the TV. The picture rolls and flickers while he squats in front of it like a frozen frog. We have a crappy old TV, and we can't afford the satellite hookup anymore. Little Harold spends equal amounts of time twiddling with the antenna and the inactive dish. Sometimes, if the clouds are just right, it sort of works, like it does tonight.

I stand there and watch my little brother watch TV.

It's a cartoon about Death the Grim Reaper. Weirdly, in the cartoon, The Bony Guy sounds like he came from Jamaica. And he's enjoying a bubble bath. Given my experience with The Bony Guy, I don't think it is very realistic, but then, gravity doesn't even work in cartoons. When a commercial comes on, I walk over and dump the bag of candy bars over Little Harold's head.

"Trick or treat!"

His smile is so big I can almost see reflections of the TV screen on his teeth.

Then I sit on the floor and watch cartoons with Little Harold. He doesn't know why the Grim Reaper talks like a Rastafarian, but it doesn't worry him. Why should it? Pretty much everybody in cartoons talks funny. That's part of the point.

The TV is working pretty good. We have candy to eat. Lots and lots of candy. I'm not actually eating my share—I got sick to my stomach almost immediately. I'm not used to eating chocolate, and I didn't eat any lunch today. I won't be eating any tomorrow, either. I spent a week's worth of lunch money on candy.

It is wrong to buy love with candy. It is wrong, and I'm really glad I did it.

. . .

It's the day after Halloween. The Day of the Dead, as Ms. (Heartless) Hart cheerfully informs us in class. She even serves cookies shaped like skulls. I pass on the cookies because they creep me out.

"No thank you."

"I think Loa's trying to lose a few pounds."

General hilarity ensues.

Score one more for Ms. (Heartless) Hart.

## Chapter 18

## Extra credit

What should you do if you are stuck on frictionless ice? Assume you are nude and there is no atmospheric resistance. While correct, the answer 'suffocate' will not earn the credit.

Two postcards in the mail.

The first is a picture of a bunch of people in a very dark room full of shadows. The faces are pale in the lamp-light. There is a man in red watching as another man writes something down. There are two little kids. The kids' faces are the brightest; they shine like full moons in the light. They look really happy, those two little kids. There is also something, I don't know what, made of copper arches. That is what everyone is focused on, that thing made of metal bands.

I turn it over.

It's Corey's half-assed messy handwriting again,

So that's how the sun works. Who knew?
Love,
Corey

And the note says:

*A Philosopher Giving that Lecture on the Orrery*
*in which a Lamp is put in place of the Sun,*
painted by Joseph Wright of Derby, 1766

It's an orrery, that's what those metal bands are all about. It is very different from Mr. Banacek's orrery, but I get it. I see how it works now.

The other postcard picture is similar, but instead of an orrery as the focus of attention, there is a white bird in a glass jar. This time, the man in red is standing in the center looking straight out of the picture, right at me. His hair is wild and silver. He looks a little crazed. He can't be Isaac Newton, and he sure isn't Einstein—I don't know who he is supposed to be. I do know that the picture is creepy. Most of the room is very dark, and one of the little girls in the picture seems to be crying.

On the back, the notes say that this is *An Experiment on a Bird in the Air Pump*, Joseph Wright of Derby, 1768.

And, of course:

I'm making arrangements for your escape,
my little cockatoo.
Love,
Corey

When I look at the picture again, it's clear that the bird in the glass jar is dead. There will be no escape. It isn't going anywhere.

. . .

When I look up the artist, this Joseph Wright of Derby guy, I find out that people used to invite scientists into their homes to give demonstrations. They would bring along an orrery and explain how eclipses happened, or they would bring along an air pump and suffocate birds in front of children, or they might bring along a body and do an autopsy as after-dinner entertainment. Sometimes they sold tickets.

To be honest, I wish I didn't know about after-dinner science.

. . .

Somewhere, on the other side of the microscope's multiple lenses, there are supposed to be tiny spheres floating and bouncing off each other. They are so small that they are unbound by gravity. I am to see them and observe their behavior. Then I will understand random motion and many other things. The only problem is, I can't see any tiny spheres. I don't want to confess this.

So I just start making things up. This is not good science. My heart is beating sideways and my hands are full of pins and needles. I drop my pencil and start sobbing. I try to stop, but I can't. My hands are shaking and I can't breathe right.

It's just too weird for everyone. If it were in the cafeteria, someone would probably try to give me the Heimlich. But I'm not choking. I'm crying. There is no first aid for crying fits.

Mr. Banacek calls the office, and then he comes and stands by me. He says my name, "Loa, Loa, are you OK?"

I try to say yes, but I don't have any breath for it.

The school nurse and the secretary from the front office come through the door. The two of them help me stand up and guide me away. Away from the tiny spheres I can't see and the students who shouldn't have to put up with this sort of shit while they are trying to learn.

I try to say I'm sorry, but that doesn't come out either.

Eventually, they get me to the nurse's room and help me remember how to breathe.

"Have you had panic attacks before?" The nurse is looking at me.

"No," I say, "Never." And it is true. I've never had anything quite like this before.

"Do you want us to call your parents? Do you want to go home?"

"No. I'm fine. I feel better. I just need to wash my face. I'd like to go back to class . . . in a little while. I'll be ready."

I need to figure out what sneaked up on me in physics. I have to go back in that classroom right away. I need to go in there and hold myself together. I may be ashamed, but I will apologize. I will ask Mr. Banacek for a practice data set so I can complete the assignment and learn what I need to learn. I will breathe slowly and I will relax the tension in my shoulders.

I can't let this happen at school ever again, and I won't.

. . .

And now it's pigs.

There's another postcard in the mailbox.

It is a photograph of four dark-haired girls dressed in pink. Pink tights, shiny pink leotards, pink gloves. They are all wearing pink lipstick and pink rubber pig noses. Their leotards are slit so you can see the row of big pink nipples running down their bodies like pig teats. There is fake blood on their throats, but it's not nearly enough if this is supposed to be about cruelty to animals. There are piles and piles of magazines. It must be hard to stand on all that slippery paper—hard to keep balanced on a great big sloping stack of paper. There are meat hooks hanging from the ceiling, and the pink piggy girls are holding onto the hooks to keep their balance.

It reminds me of a bizarre setup on a reality show. The judges for the modeling contest are going to scold them all for porny poses—like they should be able to wear giant pink nipples and still be able to sell the shoes without making it about sex. After the scolding, the girl on the left is going to get voted off because she isn't connecting with the camera.

I'm drinking absinthe in Prague.
Wish you were here.
Love,
Corey

Really, he wishes I was there? Dressed like a murdered pig?

I want to think that I understand what is going on, but I don't really. Why is Corey sending me this kind of mail?

. . .

There are two web addresses on the back of the card, but when I check them on the library computer, they both come up 404, File Not Found.

Part of me just wants to throw the postcards in the stove and burn them up—problem solved. Part of me thinks they are pieces of information. I'll need them somehow.

All of me wishes I never had to open the mailbox again, but I'm afraid what will happen if I don't. I don't want Mom or Dad to see what might show up next. I don't want to have to explain what I can't explain.

. . .

I used to enjoy chopping wood. It used to feel good to bring the maul down and split the round open. I liked using the ax to cut the pieces smaller. I liked using the hatchet to cut the smaller pieces into kindling. It is satisfying and analytical to just bust the problem into smaller and smaller pieces. It is mental, not just physical; you have to read the wood, see where it wants to split. Then I liked gathering up everything and taking it inside to the woodbox and seeing it there. I liked using it to build fires to keep us warm.

I used to enjoy it, but now the ghosts of Mom's murdered chickens haunt the area.

I turned the chopping block over so I couldn't see the bloodstains, but I know the blood is there. I picked up the little amputated chicken heads with their open beaks and surprised little chicken tongues and buried them in a deep hole with the chickens the weasel killed. I piled rocks on the spot so some woodland opportunist didn't dig them up and drag them around. The case should be closed, but I don't enjoy chopping wood anymore.

I still have to do it. I just don't enjoy it.

That pretty much describes everything anymore.

. . .

Two postcards again, from Rome. At first the pictures just look like ugly architecture. The kind with too much frosting and not enough cake. Then I see. It isn't a room decorated with plaster and gold leaf. It is a room full of bones. The arches are made of leg bones and skulls. Circles of pelvises and vertebrae are orbiting the ceiling. One postcard even includes whole skeletons dressed in brown robes propped up along the bony walls. Their skulls are bowed, and their bony little hands are hidden in their sleeves. I wonder how the skulls are attached. If they come loose, would they roll along the floor? Or would they shatter like eggshells?

I just do not want to look at that. So I shove the postcards into my pocket and start walking, fast, up the hill toward home. I try not to remember what they looked like, the skeleton puppets in brown dresses. I am not successful.

It is very hard not to remember something. It's easy to forget but very hard not to remember on purpose. Maybe I should try to forget the irregular French verbs I'm supposed to know by Friday.

I know that I can't choose not to remember. I can't choose the slide show in my imagination.

I can practically hear my own neurons laughing at me. The little shits.

My brain is not my friend.

Corey is not my friend.

French irregular verbs are not my friends, either.

. . .

I'm cleaning up after dinner, standing by the sink rinsing out a cloth so I can wipe off the table and counters.

I hear Dad say, "It ain't working."

I go in the other room to see if he is talking to me. Maybe I can fix whatever wasn't working. Maybe the two of us together can make it right.

Dad isn't talking to me. He's staring at the wall. There aren't even any pictures of dead ancestors there. He's just staring at a blank place on the wall. "Not working," he says again, "Not working."

There are a couple of possibilities here:

1) Dad is talking to himself. OK. People do that. Except Dad doesn't. It isn't his way.
2) Dad is talking to people who aren't there. Not so OK. That might be more of a problem.

Whatever is wrong, I don't know how to fix it. I don't know how to make it work.

. . .

*Someone is trying to frighten us by tampering with photos of my father's funeral. In some of the photographs, there is blood on the face or neck of the man who is supposed to be my father in the dream. In some of the pictures, he is propped upright in the* casket, but not exactly straight. He's leaning to the point where he might fall out and onto the floor.

When I turn the page in the photo album, the pictures just go on and on: pictures of my dead father at his funeral.

Every time I turn a page, the pictures get weirder and weirder. In one of them, my father is encased in a papier-mâché cocoon with a lumpy, blotted shape and winglike appendages. There are smears of blood and feathers on the outside of the cocoon. I can't see my father, but I know he is in there, under all that glue and newspaper.

I try to explain to my dream mother. I say, "Someone is trying to hurt us." But I can't find the pictures that have been altered. They are missing from the album.

When I check to make sure that my dream Little Harold is OK, I see him outside. He is having a tea party. He is using the bloodstained chopping block for a table.

I am really, really afraid.

## Chapter 19

## Field of View

The field of view (area of visible image) is an important consideration when selecting your telescope. In general, the greater the magnification, the smaller the field of view.

Both rigs, Mom's crappy little Nissan wagon and Dad's truck, are parked in front. Given their work schedules and everyone's natural aversion to misery, this is weird. There must be some new craptacular emergency. I don't even want to consider the possibilities.

I avoid the kitchen door. I walk around to the creek-side porch of the house.

When I reach the porch, it isn't weirdly quiet. That's a relief. Dead people don't make noise. And there isn't a screaming argument punctuated with breaking dishes. No domestic dispute in progress.

The TV is on in the living room, but the room is empty. I just stand there for a moment with the door open. I'm home, but whatever is happening isn't my problem yet. I'm still between one state and another: knowing and not knowing, live kitty and dead kitty.

The fuzzy picture on the TV starts to flip and roll.

Little Harold blasts out of the kitchen fast as a garter snake with legs, "Ice-cream-a-ganza!" he yells.

It takes a minute to process his news. Especially since he piles into me so hard he almost knocks me on my butt. I think it is supposed to be a hug. Then he grabs my hand and drags me toward the kitchen.

We used to have ice-cream-a-ganzas when Asta was alive. We would eat ice cream for dinner and celebrate lesser-known holidays like First Buttercup Day or the Solemn Remembrance of the Last Yeti.

We haven't had an ice-cream-a-ganza for a very long time.

"What are we celebrating?" I ask when I step into the kitchen.

"Your mom is going to the university," says Dad.

He and Mom have dishes of melting ice cream in front of them. They also have Pokémon juice glasses full of Wild Turkey 101. Judging by the level in the bottle, they have been paying more attention to the whiskey than the ice cream.

"Sit down, Loa," says Mom, "It's an ice-cream-a-ganza."

"Ice-cream-a-ganza," says Little Harold. "We have Moose Tracks and Pumpkin. Do you want Pumpkin?"

"Pumpkin sounds good." I know Moose Tracks, loaded with peanut butter and chocolate, is Little Harold's favorite. Pumpkin is better than it sounds, anyway.

"I'm going to school," says Mom.

That confirms what I thought I heard. Those are the words. What the hell they mean, I don't know that.

"Your mom is smart. It's time she went to school," says Dad.

I could use a little of that Wild Turkey, but I settle for a scoop of ice cream. "Wow," I say.

"You kids and your mom will be moving into town. That'll make it easier. I'll be staying here, to keep an eye on things, to make sure the pipes don't freeze," says Dad.

"Like, when? Next September?" By next September, the ice cream will be long gone and this particular plan will probably be long forgotten. A lot can happen in a year. A year ago, Esther was alive. A year ago, I was winking at Corey during debate practice.

"You'll be moving during Christmas vacation. She's going to be starting in the middle of the school year," says Dad.

"Wow! Does she have time to take the tests and write essays and do all the other paperwork?" I wish I hadn't said that. I'm afraid I might have broken the spell and now everything is going to unravel. If I'd kept my mouth shut, maybe we could have been happy, all of us, for one night at least. Or as long as the ice cream and whiskey lasted, anyway.

"They have this thing called 'conditional acceptance' for older students. I'm already conditionally accepted. I'm in. If I don't get at least a C+ average, then I need to take some tests. But I'm not worried. I think I can pull that off," says Mom.

"Your mom is smart," says Dad again, and he smiles into his Pokémon glass full of whiskey.

"Your dad used the land as collateral and took out a bank loan to tide us over until my financial aid comes through and I get a part-time job," says Mom.

Until this very moment, I thought college financial aid was like welfare. I assumed that my parents disapproved of it on principle. Welfare is something our family doesn't do. We never got any help with Asta's care, so I can't wrap my head around them thinking financial aid is acceptable.

We don't accept welfare, we don't buy shit on credit, and we don't eat anything with paws. I thought those were the rock-hard truths about this family, about who we are, but I may need to fiddle with the focus a little more. "We" may not be exactly who I thought. And that leaves "Me" a little fuzzy around the edges, myself.

. . .

It has been a long time since I climbed to the roof of the woodshed. I used to do it all the time when I was Little Harold's age. The woodshed roof was my observatory then. Dad called it my castle and laughed about me being the princess of the kingdom, but he was wrong. I wasn't any boring old princess. I was a star watcher. Mom used to save the cardboard tubes from the inside of paper towels and give them to me. I used them for telescopes.

It's a fine example of little-kid weirdness, a cardboard tube telescope. The stars never looked any bigger or brighter. All it really did was limit the size of the sky.

But tonight the sky is bigger than I've ever seen it. It almost makes me dizzy, and it feels like the stars are rushing at me. I wish I had the security of a cardboard tube in my hand. Maybe, instead of looking at the sky, I would look at our house and my family in it. I think I might see a lot of things I've completely overlooked.

The woodshed roof is Little Harold's territory now. I don't know what stories he tells himself when he is up here. Dad calls him Tarzan. And he strung up a zip-line cable from a tree by one corner of the woodshed to the barn. I don't know if Little Harold thinks he is Tarzan, but he spends hours skimming through the air and then dragging the pulley back to the woodshed for flight after flight.

I've never tried it. I know it will hold me, because Dad tried it the first day he put it up, but I've never tried it. Tonight, though, it seems like the way to go, so I reach out and grab it and lean forward. Then I'm rushing through the dark. I'm a shooting star.

. . .

The guy who shows us our family housing apartment has two things to say, and he says those two things over and over. One message is that we were very lucky that the place had opened up when we needed it and that we qualified to be first on the waiting list for that particular residential option. The other message is that he was sorry it isn't nicer, cleaner, bigger, or more conveniently located to the laundry, parking lot, or playground. I get the feeling he is used to hearing a lot of complaints.

We don't care.

I can clean a house. It won't take long.

He says we can paint if we want to, but only if we get paint from the manager's workshop. The approved colors are bone white, navaho white, antique white, and vanilla. He isn't sure which of those colors are on the walls already. The difference between bones and vanilla is pretty subtle, I guess. We can get paint chips for comparison at the manager's workshop. He has to emphasize that we are only permitted to use the approved colors. He looks at us and taps the wall for emphasis. Antique-vanilla-bone-blank it is. So much for my evil plan to paint everything truck-stop-bathroom green or eggplant-milk.

After he makes sure that the kitchen faucet really drips and it isn't just not-quite-turned-off, he says good-bye and leaves us to explore our new habitat.

"Cable!" yells Little Harold, "We have cable." He picks up the black wire and stares into the widget on the end like he can already see the wonders of KartoonLand.

"Don't get excited," I say, "It doesn't work if you don't pay the company."

"Don't get excited," says Mom, "There are people living below us and on both sides. It's not like at home. Take your boots off and stop jumping around. But we *do* get cable, just basic cable, just like we get water and garbage pickup. We only have to pay for power and phone."

There are two bedrooms. Mom gets the small one and Little Harold gets the even smaller one. I will sleep in the living-dining-kitchen area. I'm OK with that. I have the entry closet as my own space, and I can sleep on a couch after everyone else has gone to bed. After we get a couch. It's a plan.

The oven is unbelievably cruddy. The tub seal needs to be replaced. The closet bolts on the toilet are loose so the whole thing rocks when you sit down. We are supposed to have the manager schedule repairs. That's what the guy said when he was fiddling with the leaky faucet. It will be faster if we just fix things ourselves. We will be outlaw toilet-bolt tighteners, even if we abide by the painting rules. It's just the way we are. At least, I think that's the way we are.

The three of us sit on the floor waiting for Dad. He is bringing our stuff in the truck so we can get all moved in today. The first truckload is the essentials, the basics. We thought we would look around and see what else we needed before we gathered stuff for a second load. Now, after seeing the apartment, it is pretty clear that one load of stuff will max this place out.

After Dad arrives, we wrestle the mattresses and bed frames in, we put the cardboard boxes full of kitchen stuff on the counter, we bring in the dresser drawers. Little Harold dumps a big box of his prized possessions on the floor of his room to mark his territory and make himself at home. Then Dad says he needs to be going. He says he has to get back to build the fire again so the pipes don't freeze.

Then he kisses my mom on her eyelids and goes.

Like I said, some great romance.

. . .

"Who wants pizza?" says Mom, "We can get one delivered."

"Delivered!" The neighbors are going to hate us. Little Harold is not used to being quiet.

"That's a yes?" says Mom. She is enjoying his happiness so much she doesn't even tell him not to yell. It's a bigger deal than it seems, that pizza. When you live in the back of beyond, delivery pizza is an alien and desirable custom. Little Harold is ecstatic. He is happy in his new home.

. . .

There are some other, minor, details I have to work out.

For one thing, I have to decide if I want to keep attending the same school. Mrs. Bishop says she can work it out if I want that, but our new address is really in the other high school's boundaries. The curriculum options are virtually the same, the schools have the same academic rating, and they even serve the same lunches. So the question is really if I wanted to start over socially.

I feel like I am going to be starting over socially no matter what. I'm going to be starting over socially for the rest of my life.

And I want to actually finish the Freak Observer thing for Mr. Banacek. All he wants is a brief definition in a couple of sentences. I don't need any extra credit. It's unfinished business. That's all.

Loa Lindgren
Physics per. 1
Extra credit/makeup assignment

## The Freak Observer (Boltzmann Brain)

The Freak Observer is a conscious entity that pops into existence in its own universe. It is hypothesized to exist because an infinite number of universes have been hypothesized to exist. Given so much infinity, it is probable that something like a naked brain floating in space just spontaneously happens.

Ludwig Boltzmann was a physicist who died in 1906. He is most famous for his formula about entropy. He lived at a time when it was assumed that there was only one universe and it had existed forever. He thought that if we observed the universe long enough, we would see the equivalent of an egg unscrambling.

New observations have led to the conclusion that the universe had a beginning, the big bang. Because the universe is still expanding, time (for us) flows in only one direction. As long as the universe keeps expanding, we will not see an egg unscramble. But since our universe had a beginning, it suggests that there might be other events, other universes, or parts of universes that also begin and end. The Freak Observer is that sort of event.

(PS: Thank you, Mr. Banacek. I learned a lot from you.)

. . .

I didn't tell Mr. Banacek that I'd been using the problem of the Freak Observer like a bunch of jingling keys to distract my brain. I didn't tell him the Freak Observer is my space suit when I'm floating in the cold and the dark. I didn't tell him that I cry for the other Freak Observers. I didn't include that stuff, because that's emotion—and emotion doesn't belong in physics.

Chapter 20

# POE
# (Process of Elimination)

When taking a multiple-choice test, it can be tempting to look for the correct answer right away. You can improve your odds by eliminating any answers that are obviously wrong.

New school, new halls, new bodies in the halls, same classes, different teachers. My locker handle doesn't need to be jiggled to get it open.

There is no waiting for the school bus, no ride home. Instead, I just walk on sidewalks, past houses and record stores and coffee shops. The snow gets pounded into dirty slush by the traffic in the streets.

I still can't figure out what the deal is as far as French spelling is concerned, but my new French teacher told us that there was a nefarious plot in the Middle Ages to make written French difficult so the riffraff couldn't learn to read and write. It may be a lie, but it is a convincing lie.

· · ·

It is The Bony Guy, and he is not even in disguise. He is standing on his crooked leg bones in a wooden coffin. A white bedsheet is flapping around him. It is whiter than his bones and whiter than the clouds in the dark sky behind him. He is looking straight out at me. Black eye sockets, a ruined hole that used to be a nose, bright little white beads for teeth. Then I see he is holding a bow with an arrow pointed right at me. So much for subtlety. I flipped the postcard over just so I wouldn't have to look at it.

Duuuude! Love, Corey

And the note: *De Dood als boogschutter*, Detail uit: *Laatste oordeel*, Hermann tom Ring, ca. 1550–1555.

I have a manila envelope in my closet. I keep the rest of Corey's postcards in there and all the other loose pieces of paper I don't want to leave behind. I add De Dood to the contents, and then I leave the apartment.

I was happy in my new home. I hoped, maybe, that The Bony Guy couldn't find me in my new hiding place. It doesn't matter, really, what I hoped or what anyone hopes.

· · ·

I like having two sharp new number 2 pencils. I like their pointy-pointy, ugly, school-bus-yellow nature. I do not like their erasers, which don't work properly. This doesn't matter, because I do not intend to make any mistakes.

I also like the cavernous lecture hall. I like sitting third row from the front. I like sitting in an aisle desk, although the desk seat is not accommodating to my ass. There is no reason to move to another desk—they all have identical plastic, butt-proof chairs.

I love my test booklet with its sealed pages.

I love filling in the little bubbles. My marks are dark and complete ovals.

This is my place. This is my comfort. The rules are clear, and it's all under control.

I'm supposed to be thinking only about *this*.

My brain is made for this.

I wish I could be taking this fucking test for the rest of my life. I like it that much.

· · ·

"Hey, Loa!"

I'm standing on the stairs outside after the test is over. I waited until everyone else was gone before I left the building. I didn't have any place I needed to be. And now the test is over, I don't have anything to look forward to, either.

"Loa!"

It is the Nice Guy who crashed into my bike last summer. How ya' doin', Nice Guy?

"So what's worse, road rash or the SAT? I almost blew it. A couple of pages in the test stuck together and I filled out like ten questions before I noticed that I was screwing up. Then my eraser worked like shit and smeared all over the place. The computer will probably gag on that. Maybe we'll all have to take the test over."

He takes a breath. He smiles.

I smile too. "That would be great. I'd like to take that test over."

"Hey, you need a ride home? Or are you riding your bike? If you are riding your bike, you are one serious bike-riding animal. It's like, uphill, for miles . . . "

"No. I live in town here, just off campus, now."

"Well, I can still give you a ride. If you want."

"I'm just going over to the university library," I decide at that moment.

"I can walk over there with you. I got a little nervous energy to burn."

Watch it, Nice Guy, that smile is going to crack your cheeks.

"Sure."

"Hey, you wanna walk through the art building on the way? There's always some weird shit in there."

"OK. If it's open."

"If it isn't open, you just have to go through the kiln yard into the pottery studio."

"That seems like weird knowledge."

"Everything I know is weird knowledge." That might sound really profound if he weren't so damn happy. Maybe he has some kind of chemical imbalance. "And coffee," he continues, "We can get some coffee."

So the next thing I know, I'm walking across campus with the human equivalent of a cartoon squirrel. I just want to satisfy my intellectual curiosity: Will he be visible to the human eye in his caffeinated state? Or will I need a quark detector?

. . .

While we are walking down the hall in the art building and I'm considering the possibility that most student artists are deeply deluded, the crazy one stops and kisses the doorknob on an office door.

"Mom-m-my," he sighs and points to the name-plate beside the door. "Dr. King is my mom. She lets me not take Ritalin. She pays for lab and clay fees so I can make my raku ducks. And she makes the best ra-men noodles in the world," He glances up and down the empty hall and whispers, "The secret ingredient is love."

OK, so *this* is not my comfort zone. I change the subject, "Ritalin?"

"It's not that I'm not pay-attentchy. I'm just not-pay-attentchy about the things that I'm not interested in. I'm just not neurotypical," says Jack

"I don't even know what that means."

"It means my brain is different." He let's that soak in for a femtosecond, "You're not so neurotypical yourself."

Score a point for squirrel-boy. He nailed that one. Judging by the cheek-cracking grin, I'm supposed to take it as a compliment. I think I will.

· · ·

Eventually we actually did make it to the Student Union to buy coffee.

"Do you have a dad?" It is an innocent question, but I regret asking it. I could be picking the scab off a big tragedy. Maybe I just rattled a skeleton awake. Even if there isn't a sorrow hiding inside the happy squirrel-boy, a question like that could trigger another public display of affection for hardware. Not for the first time, I wish I could rewind time.

"Well, if my mom were a parthenogenic whiptail lizard, I'd be a girl. . . . You know, those self-impregnating lizards that bite themselves in the side and then reproduce clonally? Well, anyway, my mom is not one, and I have a dad. He does stream reclamation after the loggers and the miners and the other evildoers mess things up. What does your dad do?"

"He's a logger."

"Perfect, as long as your dad keeps destroying the world, my dad will keep fixing it back up," says Jack, and then he starts singing. . . .

*Oh, give me a home*
*Where the logging trucks roam*
*And the ducks and amphibians play*
*Where seldom is heard*
*A discouraging turd*
*And the water's not toxic-ic-ic and grey.*

Maybe it would be better if he stuck to kissing door-knobs. It's quieter.

"Can I give you a call sometime, Loa?"

"I don't have a phone," I say. "I mean, we have a phone, but it's not mine. I'm not usually around a phone, that's what I mean. I don't have a phone. Phones bug me." Why do I feel like I need to apologize for not having a phone? People lived for centuries without phones. And maybe my life is easier without one.

"That's OK. You can call me. Here's my card. I made it in graphics class. I've been wanting to give it to somebody." He pulls a little white card out of his wallet.

It looks like a business card all right. It is the right shape and the right size. It has a name on it.

JACK KING-FISHER

How could I forget a name like Jack? How could I forget a name like King-Fisher? It must be true: lack of sleep impairs memory.

There is a bright blue squiggle in the corner of the card that looks a lot like a kingfisher, actually. It's a bird scribble. And then it says some other things too:

WEB DESIGN
RAKU DUCKS
UNDISCOVERED TALENTS

"Thank you. That's a nice card. Good logo."
"Got an A."
"I'm impressed." And I was. I really was.

Chapter 21

# Les Étoiles Filantes:

shooting stars, meteors—"Elle a vu l'étoile filante."

It's a gray Friday afternoon, and I have nothing to do. Mom and Little Harold have gone to visit Dad. I didn't feel like going, and nobody made a big deal about it.

I don't feel like being alone, either.

I dump out my manila envelope full of miscellaneous.

There are the postcards from Corey. A girl who drove a nail through a guy's skull. Four pink piglet-girls with bloody throats. After-dinner science and a suffocated bird. Piles and piles of bones made into architectural gingerbread. I don't even want to look at the other one.

I don't know why I don't throw the things away.

I guess it's because I keep thinking I'm going to figure out why Corey put pictures of the two of us out there for the whole world to see. I just want to understand why he wanted to hurt me. What the fuck did I ever do to him to set him off? Why does he keep picking the scabs off my sores? The postcards are the only evidence I have to work with, but they don't tell me much.

I'm not looking for the postcards. I just drop them back in the envelope until I can figure them out.

There is the brochure for University of California–Santa Cruz.

I don't know why I keep that either.

For just a little bit more than my dad ever made in a good year, I could pay a year's tuition. Meanwhile, my family could live in a culvert and eat stray cats. Still, it's amazing, UC–Santa Cruz. Apparently the Pacific Ocean really is turquoise blue, redwood trees really are enormous, and people get degrees in astrophysics. Then I guess, they take those degrees in astrophysics and live in a culvert and eat stray cats. Nobody I know has a degree in astrophysics. I have no clue. I put the brochure back in the envelope.

I find what I'm looking for: Jack King-Fisher's business card. I dial the number.

"Tell me about raku ducks," I say.

"Raku ducks are made of fire and can swim in volcanoes. I know all about raku ducks. What I don't know is who I'm talking to—you don't sound like Mom. Mom, do you have a cold?"

"No, Jack. This is Loa. Not your mom."

"Good. I hate it when Mom gets a cold. She drinks garlic tea. The whole house smells awful when she does that."

"I don't have a cold. I wanted to know about the ducks. Are they just imaginary?"

"No. They're real. I make them. Want to see them?"

"Yes."

"Meet me by the kiln yard on campus in half an hour. I can show you."

So I put on my coat and leave the house. I walk a little too fast, just to keep warm, so I end up getting there early and end up shivering and waiting by the gate to the kiln yard.

A guy with long red dreads is knocking bricks together. He notices me and waves me over.

"Want to give me a hand? I got to get these bricks cleaned off so I can build the door up tomorrow."

"OK."

It isn't that hard, really, to get the bricks cleaned up, but it isn't pleasant either. The bricks are really rough, and I can feel tiny cuts starting to sting. They would probably hurt worse, but my hands are so cold that they are a little bit numb.

"Nice to see you, Arno." It's Jack King-Fisher, arrived at last. "Did you already meet Loa, then?"

"Well, she didn't introduce herself, but I put her to work," Arno the red-dread-haired brick cleaner sticks a hand out for shaking. His hands are a lot rougher and warmer than mine.

"She's here to learn about raku ducks. Maybe you could show her how you throw," says Jack, "It's cool watching him throw," now Jack is talking to me, "I can't throw worth shit, but Arno is the man with the skills."

Arno seems pretty laid back, especially in contrast to Jack the cartoon squirrel. Arno scratches the reddish fuzz of whiskers on his chin and thinks it over.

"I could throw something," says Arno, "I was gonna do some stuff anyway."

Arno leads the way through the gray metal door into a huge, very warm room. It feels good, all that warm. Then we pass through into an even bigger room that smells like dust and mud. For good reason. It is a room full of clay: clay in buckets, damp clay sculptures under plastic film, muddy footprints on the floor, and everywhere dust.

It is oddly comfortable to be in a place that dirty. It is honest dirt, working dirt, not accidental. When Arno hands me a gob of gray clay the size of my head, I like the way it feels. The clay is cold and heavy and firm, but when I push my thumb into it, it relents; it gives way and leaves a hole the exact opposite of me—right down to the thumbprint of my anti-self.

. . .

Working with clay is hard, physical labor. Like chopping wood but with no chicken ghosts. Being strong is just part of it, though. There is a whole lot to know about mud as it turns out.

I watch Arno make bowls. He draws a wire through a big lump of clay–half, half, half—now there are eight smaller chunks of clay, and he slaps each into a sphere. Then he sits at the wheel. I see how the wheel works. Kicking the heavy bottom disk stores and returns the energy. This is simple physics. Arno slaps a ball down. Under his hand, it is a dome, a disk, a torus, a honey pot for Pooh, a beehive, a bowl. He pulls the wire along the bottom and then lifts the bowl away, carefully, like it is the nest that holds the last hummingbird eggs in the world. Arno makes seven small bowls, one after the other, each one almost perfectly like the others.

The eighth ball of clay is for me. When I try to sit at the wheel and do what Arno did, the clay pulls out of my hands and refuses to be a bowl. It isn't such simple physics. It isn't just strength. I'm plenty strong. It is being centered. Arno is centered. The clay just opens up into a bowl for Arno because he is the man with the skills.

After I have accomplished nothing, we carry Arno's bowls into a room that smells like a root cellar. The walls are lined with open wooden shelves. Arno lifts away a sheet of heavy plastic draped over vague lumps. There are more bowls. It's a bowl army. Waiting in the dark for the new recruits.

Then Jack moves aside little scraps of plastic and shows me his ducks. When he places one in my hand, my hand tells me it is a rock from the bottom of the creek. That is just the way it feels, heavy and cold and damp. Then I trail him outside to another shelf on an aluminum rack. He hands me a pale pinky gray duck. It is smaller and lighter. It has been through a kiln fire, and even the memory of water has been driven away. Finally, the finished ducks. They smell like smoke. Places on them shine blue and green like the feathers of real ducks. Other places are black as burnt wood.

Jack shows me how he makes his ducks, and I make a little one too. Mine doesn't really look like a duck, not the way Jack's clay birds do. I can't figure out exactly what it is that makes the difference. It might be the way he squishes the clay into the shape of the head. Maybe it is the way he licks his thumb and uses his own spit to smooth out the places that are lumpy looking. It might be the way he pokes a pencil in to make the eyes—and then the new duck is suddenly looking out at the world. Jack is the master of clay ducks. That is evident.

I have to wait to learn more about raku ducks. It's a process. I have finished step one. I have a gray, sort of duck-looking gob of damp clay to prove it.

On the way out of the studio, Arno pulls a brick out of one of the controlled infernos.

"Look in," says Arno, "Look in until you can see something."

I'm looking, but I don't know what, if anything, I'm seeing besides fire and heat.

Then Arno looks in through the little brick-sized hole into the fire, then Jack.

"Not at cone 10 yet," says Jack.

"Nope," says Arno.

I look again, but I still don't know what I'm supposed to see—or not see, since it isn't yet, whatever it is.

Arno slides the brick back into the hole.

"I'll be back when you tear down the door," says Jack.

· · ·

I walk home really dirty and tired. I'm pretty sure I can sleep without dreams.

I'm almost right.

I take a shower and I sleep hard, so hard I never wake up when Mom and Little Harold come home, even though they probably turned on the light.

· · ·

*I know I am dreaming. I came to see Arno in the kiln yard. There are lots of kilns. I think it is snowing, but when I hold out my hand, the flakes don't melt. It is ashes, falling like snow.*

*I look out the kiln-yard gate toward the river, toward the mountains. The ash storm is happening there too. It is happening everywhere.*

*"I came to see the ducks," I say to Arno.*

*He shakes his head, but it is just to shake the ashes off his dreads. The ash snow is falling really fast. I can hear a snowplow out there somewhere.*

*"Yah, mon, the ducks," says Arno. He reaches out and pulls a brick out of the door on a kiln. Then he reaches his whole arm inside the fire. When he pulls it out, he is holding a duck, but the meat is all burned off his hand and his arm. He holds the duck, and it's glowing like lava, red hot. Then he throws it into the sky.*

*Suddenly, the sky is clear. It's night and the ash storm clouds are gone. I can see the Milky Way. I can see the Pleiades, but they are very bright, brighter than Aldebaran, the eye of the Bull. Then I see the duck; it is still red hot; it is flying away into the sky.*

*"When the ducks get tired, they turn into meteors—or real ducks, sometimes they turn into real ducks. Mostly, they burn up on reentry," says Arno, but it isn't Arno. It's The Bony Guy.*

*"Why don't you just leave me the fuck alone?"*

*"If I go away, there won't be any more shooting stars."*

*"You're full of shit."*

*"And shooting stars."*

When I wake up, I'm not really scared. Disturbed, yes. Angry, a little. But mostly I want to remember what I saw—how big and bright the stars were and how the little fire duck flew away on really fast wings, the way real ducks fly.

Chapter 22

# Threat Simulation Theory

Why do we dream in the first place? Why did dreaming evolve? One theory is that we dream to practice our response to dangerous events. The role of the brain is to provide safe simulations so the dreamer can sharpen the skills needed to survive. In evolutionary terms, being able to respond to a predator in a dream could have prepared the dreamer for such an encounter in waking life. Your nightmares may be an inheritance from an ancestor able to escape from a cave bear.

I did not, ever, expect to see Corey's mom sitting at our kitchen table talking to my mom.

They are drinking coffee and flipping through some papers.

Mom looks up where I'm standing with the door wide open.

"Hi, Honey, shut the door." Mom is smiling.

The only reason I can come up with for this visit is that Corey's mom is here sharing news about pool-table sex pics. This is the day that the other boot drops and the shit hits the fan. But Mom's emotional response to discovering that I'm a porn star is not what I expected.

"Hi, Loa," Corey's mom is all cheerful and nice too.

I have no idea what is going on.

"Ms. Thompson . . ."

"Kate," interrupts Corey's mom.

"Kate. Kate is helping us with some options for the land."

"If you can talk your dad into selling the whole thing in one big piece, I think I can get him a much better price. I know people who would pay a fortune for a place like that." Then she turns to Mom and says, "Any questions? You can always call me anytime."

"Everything seems pretty clear," says Mom, "You've been a great help, Kate."

"Loa," Kate swivels around to look at me again, "I have something for you in the car. It's something from Corey."

So I follow her out to the car. We are Prius people, I see. I'm glad we aren't Ram truck people, but I don't think we are Prius people. Maybe she needs another vehicle—a beat-up pickup with an ignition problem, maybe—for visits to "clients" like us.

"Here you go. Corey kept reminding me that you were supposed to get this, but . . . you know how it is," Kate, also known as Corey's mom, hands me a cardboard box with the top taped shut.

"That's his e-mail address on the Post-it," she points to the little yellow scrap on top, "He'd love to hear from you, Loa."

Oh-yeh-sure-ya-betcha.

"He's been sending me postcards. 'Wish you were here,'" I say. I'm sure he'd love to get a message from me . . .

Corey!!!! Wish YOU were HERE. I want to strangle you with my bare hands and scratch out your entrails with my toenails and replace them with biting weasels.
LOL, LOVE, LOA

"Postcards? 'Wish you were here.' Isn't that funny and sweet? He's doing so much better," Kate says. She takes a deep cleansing breath and shakes her hair, "He loves that school. They do a lot of traveling. He thinks he might want to go into international contract law. It costs a fortune, that school, but it's worth it. He just didn't belong

*179*

here. He hated all this," she waves her hand. The gesture covers the town, the mountains, the wide gray sky, and me. . . . She may not have meant it, but she made me part of all this that Corey hated.

"Well, buh-bye, sweetie. Make sure you write to Corey. And remind your dad about what I said. An undivided acreage like that—I have great clients just waiting for something like that to come on the market."

"Thanks," I say. Thanks for the mystery box. Thanks for reminding me that I'm not what Corey wanted. Finally, thanks, but no thanks, as far as pressuring my dad to sell his home. It's not my decision, but I think it might kill him if he traded himself for money.

When I get back inside, my mom is still sitting at the kitchen table, but she has gone back to her homework.

"Can you explain what this means?" she says as she jabs at an open book with a fat yellow highlighter.

"Maybe," I say. Then I turn to put the box into my closet.

"What is that? In the box?"

"I don't know. Debate stuff from last year, probably."

"Well, come and look at this. It makes no sense."

When I sit down beside her at the table, she smiles and pushes the book over near me.

"It's good to have a live-in tutor," says Mom.

It's nice to see her happy. And she is totally right, that book makes almost no sense. Between the two of us, though, we will figure it out.

Mom and Little Harold are at the campus gym. Most days, the two of them make a trip to go swimming or run laps. Mom's not used to sitting around all day, and an hour or so of exercise calms my little brother down a bit too. It sure reduces the noise he makes when he gallops around in the apartment. I like to think that the neighbors downstairs appreciate the effort.

Since they are gone, I open the big box that Corey's mom brought into my life.

There is a book wrapped in newspaper with "Happy Birthday! I know you'll love this!" scrawled across it in black marker. When I tear away the newspaper, I recognize the cover. Corey has given me a copy of *Wisconsin Death Trip*.

The book isn't quite as I remember it. There is a baby in a coffin in a long white gown, but there is also a baby with a bottle. That one is also wearing a long white gown, but it is alive. So the book isn't full of dead babies and outlaws. There are plenty of photos where everyone is alive: four young people are sitting in a hammock, a woman with a snake in each hand and another wrapped around her shoulders, a family and their dog are sitting in front of a house. All absolutely alive.

Then I notice that Corey hadn't given me a copy of the book I saw in the library; he's given me the library's copy. He checked it out before he left for Europe, and it has been sitting in a cardboard box since then. It's about a year overdue. Assuming he checked it out and didn't just figure out some charming way to steal it.

Next, there is a little tiny bundle. It's a spanking-new MP3 player complete with charger. When I pop in the buds, the song is about the girl on the stairs who jumps because someone says they will catch her, but they don't. It was the first song I ever heard with Corey, but that's just a coincidence. The player is on random shuffle. It isn't like Corey knew what song I was going to hear.

The box is mostly full of folded clothes: my killer-bitch debate ensemble, complete with the tall black boots, and a couple of plain white T-shirts I used to sleep in when I spent the night, a single pink and black striped sock. One of the boots has a bottle of pear vodka stuffed into it.

So that's it. Here are my lovely parting gifts, the stuff Corey wants me to have, the stuff he packed up especially for me before he left me behind. I put everything but the book back in the box. Then I push the box back into the corner of my closet by the front door.

. . .

It's time to take *Wisconsin Death Trip* back to the library.

What does a person say when they return a book that's a year overdue?

I have decided to say that I found it in the closet. Maybe the previous tenant had overlooked it when he went away. That's the story I plan to use.

As it turns out, I don't have to tell anybody anything. The guy at the circulation desk just takes it and plops it on a pile of books on one of the desks. He smiles and says thanks. Transaction over. No need to deploy my well-planned, convincing lie. Life is simpler than I give it credit for being.

. . .

Since I'm in the library anyway, I read. I read about Japanese pottery. I read about careers in astrophysics. I read part of a book about dreaming and the brain.

There is a term for knowing you are dreaming while you are doing it: *lucid dreaming*. Some psychologists try to train people to do it as a treatment for nightmares. The method is to think about how to alter the dream before sleeping. The point is to imagine a "triumphant ending" to the dream story. The conclusion of the investigation is unclear. Maybe lucid dreaming reduces nightmares; maybe it doesn't.

Assuming that I could learn to be a lucid dreamer and assuming that I could control my dreams, it might be the silver bullet that puts an end to The Bony Guy. What would a triumphant ending be? I stay and win the cake in the cakewalk, and I take it home and share it with Asta? Is that a happy ending? It doesn't feel like one. What exactly is a better ending for the dream where Dad is dead? Does he burst out of the *papier-mâché* shell—ta-dah!—followed by Mom's chickens, alive and whole and not made into soup? And what about the shooting stars and innocent ducks? If I get rid of The Bony Guy, do I lose them too?

## Chapter 23

## Schrödinger's Cat: The PETA Prohibition

In 1935 Erwin Schrödinger created a little thought experiment. Imagine this, we put my cat in a steel chamber with a Geiger counter, a speck of radioactive material, and a vial of poison. Then we can observe atomic indeterminacy by observing the macro results, catwise. The Copenhagen Interpretation pushes this a little further: the cat is both alive and dead until the chamber is opened and the cat is observed to be either alive or dead. The PETA Prohibition says you don't dare put the cat in a dangerous situation like that in the first place.

There is a little box on the kitchen table. It is addressed to me. It is from Europe, and I don't want to open it. I suppose I should trust that Homeland Security would have caught it if it were a bomb. It doesn't buzz, so it isn't killer bees.

The phone in the kitchen rings.

"Aloha, Loa. Hey, you better not go to the University of Hawaii, because that would be really irritating. Aloha, Loa. Aloha, Loa."

"Jack, is that you?"

"Who else?"

"Well, lots of people use phones, Jack. For example my mother usually answers this one. She would find your behavior confusing, and she would probably hang up right away."

"Good to know, but you really shouldn't go to Hawaii. Unless you use your middle name. Do you have a middle name?"

"It's Elizabeth, Jack, my name is Loa Elizabeth."

"That would work. It isn't as cool as Loa. Aloha, Elizabeth. Maybe it wouldn't work. Does your mom call you by both names when you screw up? Because Aloha Elizabeth could make you feel like you screwed up."

"Jack, did you have some reason for calling me? Other than warning me about Hawaii?"

"Want to see a movie? Want to see *Mah Nakorn*? It's playing at the campus theater."

"Monocorn? Is that like a unicorn?"

"No. *Mah Nakorn*. Two words, with a *K*. It's from Thailand. In English the title is *Citizen Dog.*"

"I don't know. . . ."

"Well, it has amputation, nosepicking, and a zombie taxi driver—it's a romantic comedy."

"OK, Jack. OK."

. . .

It is a good movie, actually.

. . .

Little Harold has opened the box. I had left it on the table, in plain sight. It's not like anyone told him not to open it.

There is some crumpled up bubble wrap beside the open box.

I can hear Little Harold in his room.

He is sitting on the floor playing. He probably doesn't admit to his friends that he still plays with his action figures and Happy Meal toys, but he does. He is just sitting on the floor playing.

He looks up at me in the doorway.

"Hi Loa, look what you got. It's cool. What is it? I was just playing with it a little bit." He holds it out to me.

"It's OK. I'm not mad. You shouldn't open other people's mail though, alright?" I say.

The thing is surprisingly heavy. And weird.

It is solid, like a sculpture, not an action figure. It looks like a hunchback bird with a funnel on its head. It has long floppy ears or wings drooping almost down to the ground. It is holding something, a letter probably, speared on its twisty beak.

"What is it?" asks Little Harold.

"I don't know. What do you think it is? Was there anything else in the box?"

"Just this," he says and handed me a folded-up postcard. "It's cool. That thing. Can I play with it again sometime?"

"Sometime, maybe, after I look at it."

"Cool," he says, and then he resumes the story in progress with the rest of the action figures and stuff.

. . .

I take the little figure and the postcard with me to the library. I typed in "jheronimus bosch," like it said on the bottom of the bird. The library catalog likes "Hieronymus Bosch" better and burps up twenty titles to consider.

I learn a few things about my weird bird. He appears in a painting, in the left panel of *The Temptation of Saint Anthony* made by Hieronymus/Jheronimus Bosch about 1550. He is wearing skates. Nobody knows for sure what the word on the letter in his beak means. And as far as weird goes, a hunchback bird on ice skates is not in the Hieronymus Bosch top ten. A walking stomach, for example, with what looks like Cubone the lonely Pokémon's ancestor riding on its back playing a harp: that's weird. A guy with feet, wings, tentacles, and hands wearing glasses. That's weird.

When I open some of the art history books, I feel like I'm reading one of those dumb dream-symbol dictionaries. Ice skates are equal to folly. Funnels are equal to the deceits of science.

It just bugs me, the idea that there is a simple answer. Maybe that's because I want simple answers. I want to know why Corey sent me this thing. I want to know if Esther knew the truck was coming. I want to know if the little lights that were Asta blinked out one at a time like stars behind a moving cloud or if they all went dark like twinkle lights as soon as one failed. I want to know she wasn't a lonely little chick brain floating without a shell.

But I don't know shit.

. . .

When I get home, I find messages for me on the table: one of those green sticky notes Mom loves to leave around and an envelope from my old high school addressed to me.

The green sticky note says, "Your friend Jack called, and your duck is ready to cook. Be at the studio tonight around seven. I hope you know what that means. Little Harold and I are swimming. Make dinner, please, we are going to be starving when we get home. Little Harold says not to cook duck—or chicken, either. Love, Mom."

I open the envelope and unfold the sheet of paper inside.

It is my extra-credit essay.

It doesn't have a score on it, but there is a note in Mr. Banacek's square-printed letters, just like he used on the whiteboard in class.

Loa, Sometimes the theory side of physics seems a little loony to me. You were an outstanding student and a pleasure to have in class. I have a lot of confidence in you. If you ever need a letter of recommendation, let me know.
T. Banacek

. . .

"So what do you know about Hieronymus Bosch?" I'm helping Arno build a kiln door while I wait for Jack.

"I make pots. I don't study history," Arno pauses and looks carefully at a brick. Then he puts that brick down and chooses another that looks exactly the same as far as I can tell. "Nobody knows anything about Hieronymus Bosch. Not really."

I pull the weird bird out of my coat pocket and hand it to him. Arno holds the figure at eye level and looks at it, "Well, one thing I can say about Hieronymus Bosch is that this image works. Whatever the hell this thing is, it's interesting." He hands my gift back to me.

"I'm glad I make pots," says Arno, "I think clay is easier to work with than nightmares."

"I read today that the town he lived in burned down when he was thirteen. Do you think that was the problem?"

"What problem? The guy was a genius. But maybe he just ate spoiled rye bread. It was full of LSD. That explains a lot about the Middle Ages. They were all hallucinating. Here, let me show you something really important."

He goes into the main studio and comes back with a fistful of sloppy clay. It stinks. It smells just this side of organic. It smells of rot and damp earth. Arno holds the ball of mud in his hand, just as he had held the bird figure earlier. He looks at it carefully. Then he pinches it and flicks it and runs his thumbs along it like his hands are looking for something.

Then he stops and plops the clay on the top row of bricks on the kiln door. It is a little wet clay gargoyle all of a sudden: a thing with expressive eyes and stooped shoulders and a fat gut.

"Kiln god," says Arno. "Put your faith in the kiln god, at least until we open the door and see how the pots came out."

. . .

I've been staring at the fluorescent lights on the studio ceiling for two and a half hours. I understand now why the place is dotted with decrepit couches. People do a lot of waiting in this place. I, for example, am waiting for Jack. He should never be a paramedic or a delivery guy or . . .

"Hey, wow, it got late," says Jack. "Maybe we should do this tomorrow, the raku. 'Cause, like, it got late."

So we walk home, and my naked unfinished duck stays where it is, pale and grainy on the shelf, waiting to be changed into something else. Its little blobby bathtub-duckie shape is starting to grow on me. Sure it looks a little inert next to Jack's ducks, but it is patient and looks more like a duck than a doorknob.

Jack and I walk across campus. The stars are out so I start naming them. Jack seems interested. At least he points his nose in the right direction and cocks his head.

Sometimes Jack reminds me a little of my old dog, Ket. Like now, when he tips his head like he is listening for the stars. I still miss Ket and the way he used to look at me like he wanted to know what I wanted him to know. It is the sort of look that can easily be mistaken for love.

"Can you really see pictures when you see the constellations?" asks Jack.

"What do you mean?"

"Can you really see pictures? Or is it more like just a shape? An abstract shape?"

"Well I guess it's more like just a shape. I guess that Cassiopeia, the Queen in her Chair, looks more like a *W* than a queen or a chair."

"How does it feel, to know them? To see them as particular stars like that?"

"I don't know. A little consoling, I guess. I never really thought about how it feels."

"Can you *not* see them, the constellations, can you just see the sky?"

I look up. There are stars I have no name for; there are stars up there that are invisible to the human eye, stars that can only be seen in the Hubble telescope mirror or heard as radio waves. But I can't "not see" the constellations that I know.

"It is sort of like reading, once you learn to read, you can't look at a word and not read it. Even if you leave out letters, your brain will fill in the places and make a word and make it make sense. The constellations are like words I know how to read. I can't 'not see' them."

It's a little surprise: Jack can be quiet. He never says another word until we get to my building and he says good-bye.

. . .

I have a French test on Monday. It hasn't gotten any easier. French makes me feel stupid. It's like I don't even have a place in my brain for *l'enfantin langage* much less *le dérègle-ment du langage*. I write the stupid stuff down over and over like Bart Simpson writing *"Je ne parle pas Français"* and it doesn't help. By this time, my hands should know it; it should be embedded in my muscle memory even if my brain is a lost cause.

. . .

*I'm trying to buy a ticket. I don't know if it is for a movie or a trip, but I can't get the attention of the person on the other side of a glass window. I think the little speaker device is broken or something. I start banging on the glass.*

*The ticket agent gestures to the side of the window. There's a tube there with a screw-on lid, like they use at the bank drive-through for deposits of cash. I want to put a note in there to explain what I need, but I don't have a pen or paper. I start rummaging through my pockets looking for something to use.*

*I find the letter that the messenger bird was carrying, but it is the real letter. I'm torn between using it for scratch paper and knowing that it is very valuable. Someone might know how to read this message. I shouldn't destroy it.*

*The lights in the lobby start to flicker out, and I realize that the ticket agent is leaving. I start banging on the glass. I need help. I need to buy a ticket.*

*An announcement comes on over the PA system. I can't understand it. It's in French. I can only understand the day of the week, "<u>Lundi</u>."*

*The ticket agent looks right at me and shrugs. Then the last of the lights go out, and I'm standing there in the dark holding a letter I can't read.*

*I look out the window, and I can see stars in the sky, they are all very bright and beautiful, but none of them is familiar.*

· · ·

It's nice actually, to wake up in the middle of the night and not be terrorized. It's nice to just wake up and wonder, "Wow, what was that?" and then feel OK about flipping the pillow over and going back to sleep.

Believe me, it's even bigger than being able to have pizza delivered.

It isn't quite so nice to wake up and find out that first period starts in less than half an hour. I never slept in before. Maybe I need to buy an alarm clock—a wind-up one with a big clanging bell on top like they have in old cartoons. How cool is that?

Chapter 24

# False Positives

A brain scan on a dead salmon produced evidence that the deceased fish continued to think and was sensitive to the emotions of human beings. Appearances can be deceiving, however. The glowing red spots on the MRI weren't signs of dead-fish empathy. They were simply "noise" generated by the equipment itself—a "false positive" result. In fact, a dead fish has exactly the same level of brain activity as a dead Cornish hen or a pumpkin, which is none at all. It looked like the lights were on, but nobody was home.

We are doing expository presentations—a.k.a. speeches with props—in English. Mine is next week, and I've just realized that my plan to bring in a freshly cooked raku duck might not pan out. I hadn't figured Jack into the equation. He isn't exactly dependable in a where-and-when sort of way. But I'm weirdly unconcerned about next week. For one thing, I could take off my boot and use it as a visual aid to explain Freak Observers. I could do that right this minute, but I don't have to. I can just sit back and be a member of the respectful audience.

Yesterday one guy explained how to make a drum out of a propane tank. That was followed by the story of Nintendo's shift from sex hotels to video games. I'm fairly confident that I would never have discovered those things on my own. I'm learning things in school.

Today the first girl talks about being an insulin-dependent diabetic. She has good, clear diagrams and seems to understand the way her body has failed her really well. She pulls out an orange and says a nurse taught her how to give herself shots when she was eleven. Now she passes the lesson on to us. It seems like she is finished, but then she picks up another syringe and says, "Just saline." She points it at the ceiling, flicks it, presses the plunger, and looks at it. She is looking for bubbles. Bubbles are bad. She pulls up her sweater and exposes her side. Her face doesn't even twitch when she sticks herself with the needle.

. . .

The next girl has dimly green hair—it looks like a bad Kool-Aid dye job—and she looks nervous. That's understandable. Unless she is going to give us tasty snacks, it is going to be hard to make us stop thinking about that needle, that needle, that needle. And she doesn't appear to have snacks.

She leans a stack of big foam-core posters against the whiteboard. She isn't showing them to us yet. That's smart. She's going for the big reveal.

Then she puts a little bundle of cloth on the table at the front of the room, takes a deep breath, and looks to the teacher. The teacher nods.

The lime-haired girl turns over her first poster.

It's The Bony Guy.

He's wearing a suit of armor, but it's him.

She flips over to the second poster.

This time, he's dressed in a brown robe, like the monks in the bone-decorated room, and it says "Saturn" by his feet instead of "Death," but it's him.

The shock is wearing off, and I'm starting to hear the words of her speech. These are Tarot cards; they are used to provide answers and guidance. She learned to read them from someone call Nonna, who is her grandmother, I gather. She collects different decks—the way some people collect manga—and she is going to explain how they work.

Now that my brain is turned back on, it is in defensive-snark mode. It doesn't pay to soak your head in Kool-Aid—I can recognize the bright red star of Aldebaran in Taurus, but I don't think it has any influence on my day. I could do my speech about astrology and include the experiment where everyone gets a random fortune, and then they have to decide if it is "correct" or not, and then everybody realizes they are fools. I am so not being a respectful audience.

Now the speaker has unwrapped a deck of cards. They are so big, it looks like she is holding a paperback—but it's a paperback where you can shuffle the pages.

She sets the shuffled cards down carefully and points to the posters again. She talks about the traditional images of death. He often carries a scythe, she says, turning over another poster to reveal a full-frontal Bony Guy dressed in Little Red Riding Hood's cape.

She says people tend to freak out when the Death card appears as part of the answer to their question. They assume it's a very bad thing. But it isn't that simple. Some decks don't even have a Death card. And a card's meaning always depends on the question and its position relative to other cards. When Death is right side up, it usually means there is some sort of change happening—a new beginning. She flips Red-Riding-Hood Death on his head. Now the card might mean that you're stuck in a rut or hanging onto old ideas that aren't working. She makes death sound like a variable.

There are all kinds of tarot decks, that's what the collector-girl with the greenish hair said.

. . .

Nobody else is home this afternoon, so I pull out my manila folder and spill out the postcards and stuff. My deck, I think.

Bony Guy-Death Card-De Dood lands upside down.

"Stuck in a rut," says gravity-defying De Dood.

Jack's business card is almost covered up by De Dood. I can see part of the bird squiggle, like it's trying to fly up and away. I'm not freaking out. There's more to reading the cards than just dumping them out. There's a system to it. I don't remember all the details, but it's about position and relationship. The answer isn't in the data; it's in the analysis.

My deck, I think, so my deal. I can shift the variables in the equation. I lift De Dood and turn him right side up and put him off to the side. Now I can read Jack's card: "raku ducks, web design, undiscovered talents."

"New beginnings," says De Dood from his new place out of the center.

What about the other cards? What is the significance of the four of pink-nipple piggies? The ace of hammers? Is that the king of after-dinner science? I didn't even know I was looking at an orrery when I first saw that card. The machine in the painting looked so different from Mr. Banecek's, the one I'd nudged a little to keep the planets moving.

I turn it over and read,

So that's how the sun works. Who knew?
Love,
Corey

Turning it again, I notice that the lamp meant to be the sun can't even be seen. It is revealed only because it reveals other things, like the observers studying the model galaxy. The faces of the observers shine like phases of the moon. Some are full, others only a crescent of light, one in total eclipse. Do they imagine themselves on the marble-size Earth while it ticks around its clockwork orbit? When the demonstration is finished and the observers walk out under the night sky, will they see the constellations—or will they imagine other observers beyond the reach of human eyes?

. . .

I turn the card over again and touch the words that Corey wrote.

If I hadn't had practice decoding his useless sloppy marks when we were debate partners, I wouldn't be able to read the words at all.

> So that's how the sun works. Who knew?
> Love,
> Corey

. . .

Who knew?

. . .

I never told Corey that I used to have a little sister. I never told him about my bad dreams. I didn't want him to know I was crazy—because, if he didn't know, then I could be something completely different when I was with him.

He isn't mocking me with The Bony Guy because he doesn't know—he doesn't know. He doesn't know that Esther was a brave pig-whacking girl and now she is dead. He doesn't know I saw her die.

He just sent me a postcard, "Wish you were here."

I read something else, written in lines that were much too dark and much too sharp. Corey never joined those dark things into constellations—I did that.

He's not a vindictive monster. He's not trying to ruin my life. When he posted those pictures on the net, it was about him, not about me. I'm just "girl with ginormous thighs on a pool table." I have no face in those pictures. I am in eclipse. It's his face that shines in the dark. His name is in the tags. Maybe he wanted someone to see those pictures and think that was what he was doing in Europe. Maybe he was just trying to confront his own enemy in his own bad dream.

He may not know about my nightmares, but I don't know his either. All those nights in the dark, close enough to feel the energy of his body, close enough to hear the sounds of his pulse if I didn't mistake it for the echo of my own—but that's the problem. I did, somehow, mistake Corey for an echo of me. I was so focused on my reflection in his eyes, on the way he let me see myself, that I never saw him at all.

So when the postcards came, I never got them, not really. I was too busy being hurt. I was too busy hurting myself. Now I'm finally getting the messages that he sent me.

He's drinking absinthe in Prague and feeling a little sympathy for me because I'm not. He's wandering through museums and seeing amazing things he wants to share with me: a chandelier made of bones, a scowling face in a painting that looks a little like me. He's just trying to keep in touch—to touch. He couldn't text me. He knows I don't have a phone—no computer, no e-mail, no social networking. He got past all those barriers. He sneaked around them in an old-timey way. He sent me postcards. He knew I was hurt, and the postcards weren't apologies, exactly; they were little gestures that kept things open and made it possible, maybe, for us to someday be friends.

. . .

*I'm in Santa Cruz wading in the ocean. I can't hear anything. There isn't any wind. I look up at the sky, and I realize I'm deep underwater. The sunlight is flickering down in little beams and sparks. I panic and my heart jerks faster, but then I look around. There are all kinds of strange things in the water. I don't know what they are, they are just floating or swimming or hovering. It is hard to see them because the light is so undependable, but what I see is unbelievably beautiful. It makes me cry, the unpredictable hovering beauty. When I start to cry, I can feel my lungs fill up with water. It feels natural. I can breathe underwater, I just never knew it before.*

*This is just another universe. And I'm its observer.*

# Acknowledgments

To Andrew Karre, my editor: In the beginning, there was chaos. Your ability to see a book in there is a little freakish.

To the book builders of Carolrhoda—including visionary production editor Julie Harman, careful reader Delores Barton, book designer Danielle Carnito, and publicist Lindsay Matvick: thank you all.

To Kate McAlpine (a.k.a. Alpinekat) and to the community-at-large of science writers: You wade out into the lagoons of science and bring back the most amazing things. I appreciate it.

To my household, both Bedlam Central and the Martian Outpost: You are interesting.people. I love you.